Wednesday

MW01152756

"Alchemy"

September 2005 Volume 1 No. 2

Featured Photographer

Halldor Enard

Edited by

Chiwan Choi, Judeth Oden, Scarlett Riley, Tim Simone & Lizzy Waronker

Saint Nick's Press
Los Angeles

Cover Photograph by
Halldor Enard

Contributing authors are members of the Los Angeles Poets and Writers Collective.
For information please contact <u>wednesdaymag@gmail.com</u>

from the editors

Welcome to "Alchemy," issue #2 of *Wednesday*. This issue is fatter and fuller than our premier, "Tourist's Idyll"—a testament not only to our continuing growth following the emphatic reception we have received in Los Angeles, but a bigger testament to the writers of this city whom we love so much, to the bloody pages that have continued to pile up on their hard desks, to their will to continue working the craft that threatens to devour them in little pieces. It's like we are holding *Wednesday* up to God and saying, "Look! Look at what we've done with the freakin' talent you have freakin' cursed us with!"

Why "Alchemy"? Because there is something wonderful and mysterious going on within the pages you now hold before you, in all these works, in the attempt to express the nearly unexpressible, in this collection of stories and poems forged into something concrete, into something felt, not as a great piece here or there, but as a collection that is constantly in progress, like Los Angeles itself. And under the bright and unrelenting sun that threatens to reveal everything, the writers are helping us discover that this is more than a City of Gold. It is a City of Alchemy.

Literature is alive in Los Angeles. Words have become the heartbeat of the city. There is just so much going on. Beyond Baroque. *Palabrazilla*. The Los Angeles Poets & Writers Collective. Tia Chucha's. *Tongue & Groove*. *Story Salon*. *Da Poetry Lounge*. *Sit 'n' Spin*. Redondo Poets. Poets of the Roundtable. 33⅓. *mo+th*. *Wednesday*…

It is with great respect, privilege, and excitement that we present this snapshot from the West Coast.

Peace.

The Editors

table of contents

carol joffe

THE MISSING O
[excerpt]

My skin was starting to itch under the wool and I could feel little beads of sweat forming between my brows. He drove through the Lincoln Tunnel with his left hand on the wheel and the right one up my skirt. My dress was suffocating me. I wanted to tear it off. My hands were clammy, my mouth packed with dry dirt. I felt entombed in my own body. I squeezed the leather armrest on the door, or whatever it was, and sat mummified. We were going to crash. I knew it. My daughters will be dropped off and no one will be there. They'll be motherless. Even if we don't crash, my husband will take them away. I deserved to be punished, but not my precious girls, not them.

He did keep his eyes on the road no matter what else the rest of him was doing. His lips were pursed now, whispering something about nipples. I looked down to see his fingers touching one side, then the other.

"Ooh," he said, "they're so hard, so big."

I couldn't tell if he thought that was a good thing or not, and since I didn't have the courage to ask, I assumed the worst, especially since he hardly spoke to me and I couldn't think of a thing to say back. He wasn't very friendly and I was beginning to feel he'd changed his mind about the whole thing and was just going through with it not to hurt my feelings.

We passed a string of gas stations, billboards, fast-food joints and seedy motels. He slowed down as though he were looking for a particular place. He screeched a right into a place that looked exactly like all the others and pulled up to the office.

"Okay, we're here," he said.

He leaned over me, two fingers on one hand tweaked my nipple while the other hand slipped under my skirt and gave the elastic on my garter belt a little tug.

"Don't go anywhere," he joked. "I'll be right back."

He got out and left me sitting there, the door on his side still open, leaving me exposed. He walked into the office; his tan slacks and expensive jacket looked out of place, like he was slumming. I could see him talking to the clerk and signing in, probably using a made up name. The clerk was way too friendly, as though he knew him. Then I got it. He's been here before. Of course. The one-two-three plans he made with me, just like that, and that weird luncheonette and then his looking for this particular place. He probably does this all the time. Maybe every day, for all I know. I can't believe I thought it was just me he wanted. Of course, why would he? How dumb can I be?

The clerk looked out in my direction. I slumped down and pretended to be looking for something under the dashboard. He pointed his finger toward the car and circled his arm around to the left. He didn't look anything like I'd have imagined. No greasy comb-over, no snotty shirt sleeve or chewed up toothpick stuck on his lip. He had neat, gray hair and wore a wool cardigan. He looked like someone's uncle. Like my husband's uncle, Bernie, actually. If anyone was, I was the sleazy one. The thought of this Uncle Bernie guy knowing just why I was here and what I would be doing made me want to disappear, be invisible, or at least go in there and explain to him that this wasn't what it looked like. Only it was. It was exactly what it looked like.

He got back in the car and slammed the door. His energy quickened, as if he wanted to get the whole thing over with fast.

"It's just around to the left," he said without looking at me.

He dropped the key in my lap. The number 104 hung from it on a grimy, gray disc. I looked at it sitting there. The grimy grey disc on my grimy gray dress. Why did he give it to me? Was I supposed to open the door? Am I not getting something? We drove around to the back, passing a row of identical red doors. A couple came out of one of them. They looked like teenagers. She had her hand down the back of his jeans and was leaning against him, strutting her stuff in a short skirt and one of those shirred, elastic tops you can't wear a bra with and platform shoes about nine inches high. No dowdy, itchy, gray wool for her. No sir! She whispered something in his ear and they giggled their heads off as they got into their car.

"Did you see her? " I asked.

He nodded.

"What do you think?"

"Cute ass," he said.

A lot of the rooms had cars in front of them. It was a pretty busy morning, I guess. I never knew so many men didn't have to work. I thought about all the people behind the red doors, doing the same thing at the same time. Well, maybe not exactly the same, but similar. I wondered what would happen if suddenly a tornado whipped through and tore all the doors off at once. He stopped the car in front of the door with a 1 - 4 in tarnished gold plate. The middle number was missing. The big O. It was probably swiped by some floozy for a souvenir.

I didn't see him get out and walk around to my side. I was starting to worry about my big O and what would happen if I didn't have one, which I most likely wouldn't. If I hardly ever did with my husband, what could I expect with a stranger? And even if I did, it would be the wrong kind, that's for sure. He'd probably consider me a dud and not call me again. Or tell me not to call him, or however it would work. But he probably wouldn't have in any case. I started to think about that girl again and what it was that made her a slut and me not a slut? I decided, you could just tell. That's all. It was as simple as that. All you had to do was look at her.

He opened my door and took the key from my lap, and instead of taking my hand to lead me out, he put it on his thigh, and then he moved it to his crotch and held it there. Oh, my g... he was... and we hadn't even gotten into the room yet. The tip of his tongue touched mine, gentle at first, then faster. He thrust its length in and out, in and out. Focus, I thought. It's happening. This is what you want. Focus. Then as suddenly as he started, he stopped. He lifted me to my feet, pushed the lock down and shut the car door. Moving me forward, his hand on my butt, we walked the few steps together to our red door; the one with our very own part of a number on it and he put the key in the lock. Will it show? I wondered. Later? In my eyes, on my body? In my words? I walked past him into the room.

He double locked the door and attached the chain. Then he walked over to the dresser and emptied his pants pockets as though he were getting them ready to send to the cleaners. First he took out all the change and put it down near the lamp, next the bills, then his key ring and put that down, carefully, all right next to each other. Then he took off his wedding band and added that to the rest. After that he took off his pants and folded them very neatly over a chair.

I walked past him to the sink and filled a plastic cup with water. My mouth was still so dry the inside of my cheeks felt stuck together. I thought about the party. Those feelings. If it only could have happened then. When I felt like that. What's wrong with me? If just for today, please, let me feel it again. All I felt was frozen. Oh my god, the baby, did I tell Glenda to freeze the bagel? What a mess I am. A big, hard-nippled mess. I must be frigid. My husband is right. I have problems. This must be what frigid is. Sweaty and frigid at the same time, that's pretty funny. There must be a joke in there somewhere. I should be taking my clothes off, too, seducing him, driving him wild. I think it's just that I need a shower. Sure, great. Right now. Take a shower. That wouldn't be a mood breaker, now, would it? I should wash at least, but the sink's right out here in the open

I watched him step out of the last of his clothes: white, cotton boxers. Boxers, no jockeys. Uncles and fathers, they wear boxers, not lovers. Lovers wear tight. Tight is sexy. Why would he wear those? Maybe it's that thing about not overheating the sperm, so you can keep them coming for a long, long time and not use them up. I remembered reading something about that. That would explain it. He plans on doing a lot of this.

He stood there in all his long, lean, beautiful nakedness; smiling at me; a wicked smile that tipped his mouth more to one side.

"Come here, you little slut," he said.

His words flooded me, melting the fingers fumbling with buttons, liquifying the legs, defrosting all the edges. He swooped me up in his arms like a bride and, with one barely perceptible move, had me under him on the bed. With the dexterity of Houdini he removed my clothes and stopped my jabbering mind. Swallowing me with his eyes, his finger tracing downward from my cheek to my mouth.

"Now," he said.

scarlett riley

ONE BLACK WING

It was never easy to smile in our home. I thought it was because we lived on top of a hill and our house was the bone collector of the neighborhood. At the very least, we were the leveler of the street. If a dog died somewhere out front, painting the underbelly of a green Toyota red, we'd hear the scream. I knew we'd never be closer to any truth than our address.

We didn't have much in the way of valuable things, but even still, every time we passed a less fortunate on the corner of Main, or a woman sipping old milk through a coffee-stirs straw in a drug store drive, Mom would say, "By the grace of God, there walk I."

She never said that about the rich. Just the poor.

I grew up worried God only paid attention to the troubles of money and hunger. Not homes as empty as ours. It wasn't until later I decided salvation hands itself to anyone who grasps. It just turned out that we were the filter of the block. That it wasn't any different than keeping score of horses on a track. Everyone who knew about us simply placed their bets and sat back, following the walking examples of how life could have treated them. Three reasons in the faces that never smiled, Mom's, my sister's, and mine, to be grateful for the way their mouths still reacted on their own. And there went Mom, pulling us by thick pink jump-ropes tied to the handlebars of two tricycles, saying, "There walk I," 'cause Sadie's pointing to a dead bird on the sidewalk. I look at one black wing still reaching for the sky.

Once when Mom was little, eight or nine, she tried to sleep at a friend's house one town over. She liked to escape her place, too. It's something we both still have in common. I imagine she played dress-up with her friend's clothes, anxious to be someone else, and every time she tells the story, she is. She reminds me how she got herself ready for bed that night; laid down next to her friend in a one room apartment I couldn't help but compare to our living room. I know her face contorts when she pauses 'cause there's a distant detail she doesn't want to share—the feel of a thick cigar smelling glove holding her mouth closed—when she's stolen out of a window. I watch her recall the dampness of a warehouse floor on her back and the warm breath of men in her left ear. As she talks I find myself trapped where that ear used to be, before any kidnapping or accident off the freeway. I try to think about there being a time when my mother wasn't afraid of what she would say when she got old.

Sadie curls up like a ball and asks her to stop telling the story. The brown spot on the left shoulder of her t-shirt suggests a stain the first wearer must have tried to remove. Ink maybe. She digs the side of her face into the low part of Mom's chest and a grey snoopy sweatshirt that hangs too far from her collarbone.

When we sat like this, we saw a sideways reflection of cars cresting the hill. Flashes of movement caught in the small dark screen of our television. And every once in a while, if the wind was strong enough, a leaf shuddered on our plant like it heard her too. I played with the end of Mom's hair and my own, winding them together like ribbon—a black and red spiral stretching from the top of a cream colored couch cushion to the brim of my forehead. I never felt closer to her, and so against my best judgment, and the kids passing by, and the upset in my stomach, I ask her to start again.

alan berman

If I read a book [and] it makes my whole body so cold no fire ever can warm me I know that is poetry. If I feel physically as if the top of my head were taken off, I know that is poetry. Is there any other way.

Emily Dickinson, as told to
Thomas Higginson (1870)

IS THERE ANY OTHER WAY

It never fails—whenever I'm walking
with a woman for a few minutes,
I notice her straighten her back,
push her chin up.
It's a reaction to me: I walk
with my head down, my neck
at an angle. My head
is a whole head
in front of my body.

I am not sure when I began using this
defeated posture. I'm shy, have always
been shy; talking to strangers
made me fearful. Now I try
too hard to impress instead of letting my faults
take care of themselves. It's as though my body is saying,
Don't worry, you're right: He's not that good,
so don't expect much. He's not worth it.

Today I was walking around my new place
trying to pace out a solution to a design problem.
This condo is all '70s mirrors: the wardrobe closet doors
are full-length reflections
of every move I take.
They see me stop short, go to the computer,
level off at the monitor, type an attempt
that wasn't paced enough, then push away on
my rolling chair and start moving again.

The walls record my gliding towards
the bathroom, stopping to grab the cordless
and the cell just in case
good news comes while I'm doing the only
truly essential things.
I am under a siege of surveillance and I'm
finally in enough emotional turmoil
to write from a cauldron of feeling.
I see myself passing the mirror
on the way from the bathroom,
picking up my journal, slipping my pen
off the back page, and moving it against the paper.
I write and then get up.

The show is the same as always,
but this time it's my father
walking by: his hunch, his
neck on two pivots, his prematurely aged visage.
He had gone gray in mid-life, but
was bent forward from my childhood.
In a photo of him holding Steve as a baby,
he didn't hunch—the same life that later
wore him down has been pulling me.

I need to stop bowing to it—living isn't my enemy
and deserves less-callous dismissal.

I take off my shirt and step towards the only
unblemished mirror, no backing shows,
and apply my back to it from the bottom up,
as though I'm unpeeling myself to it.
My skin feels the cold of it, better than
any heat on a freezing day, better than the metallic chill
when I lean my forehead on a urinal's top pipe
while I let my fear drain from me.

MOTO PERPETUO

Almost I fear to think how glad I am.
(R. W. Emerson)

Whenever I feel this hopeful,
I can't help also feeling
that I will be the one of all my friends
to meet an untimely end.
I review the congress of deaths
and consider their causes: the bizarre ones
promise to relieve my statistical anxiety.
But there's only one, a hemophiliac
who got AIDS in the '80s from a transfusion,
before they knew any better.
But that one doesn't count:
he had a preexisting tendency towards
such an exit, and I don't.

My friend David should be dead,
but somehow persists, 30 years after his
brain tumor
(the size of—as they always are—a golf ball)
was removed, and after the three-month coma
that followed, after which he woke up,
asked for a hamburger, then lost the ability
to speak and had to begin to relearn it, during
which time he saw his mother
die from cancer caused by the fertility
drug that enabled her to beget him
and provide him his tumor;
after a dozen surgeries more
on his brain and spine
to relieve pressures and misalignments
and mistakes made in previous interventions;
after managing somehow to marry
a pretty girl from school who turned out
to be a schizophrenic, more disabled, perhaps,
in her way than he in his, so much so that
for months she could not drive him in their
van, specially modified to accommodate his
200 lb. electric wheelchair;
after spending 14 months in recovery
from a surgery with only two visits

from her; after he appeared at the door to his
doctor's office on the second floor of the
suites near the hospital for his final
checkout exam, backed up deliberately
to get a better angle on the door
(they're always so hard to open from a chair),
made one more zigzag forward and back
to get it just right (because everything
that could be, had to be just right for David),
then pitched the control handle just wrong, just
back for too long, then hurled himself down
the stairwell behind him, landing at the
landing, the wheelchair on him,
he was broken and besieged.

But this was his life,
the way that working in a dead-end job
at Target is someone else's life, or
being a concert pianist, or
counting lies made by strangers.

He has become a student of his own conditions,
and takes anti-depressants to monitor his sarcasm
and marshal his sense of the absurd
to prevent him from flinging himself
down the stairs on purpose. He is, he says,
"pretty much a quadriplegic these days."

So it came time, after all this time, to call him
to tell him the latest news. "David," I said,
"Since we're working on this 30-year reunion
and it's probably going to come up at some point,
I figured I'd better tell you now: My wife and I
have been having problems and
we have been trying to work them out,
but we finally decided that the best thing
to do is separate, so we're breaking up."
David continued in step, calm as snow:
"Same here," he said.

lizzy waronker

LURKER IN THE STACKS
[excerpt]

The books I read smelled dank like I was the first person in forever to touch them. I looked at the check-out histories in the back covers. Strangers with the same demento interests as me. The books were obviously not very popular at the lending desk because there were only a few pathetic names scrawled there in blue and black and red ink, but the pages were fingered and worn, and I knew someone had been looking at them. There were even booger smears and droplets of coffee (or blood? I hoped so, at least) on some of them, and little scribbles in the margins. Sammy's 5:30 fix car write 500 word essay toilet paper. No check-out history, not really, but boogers and scribbles and underlines, and it was obvious what I had in my hands was a stack-read. The dirty little books everyone was too embarrassed to check-out, but that everyone wanted to look at. In certain circles, like the ones Ma probably thought she traveled in, stack-reads would consist of things like *The Anna Nicole Smith Story* or *You'll Never Eat In This Town Again*, low brow crap with lots of gossip and black and white pictures in the middle section that always seemed to start falling out after one or two handles. In Nana's circle, stack-reads might be something having to do with sex, like *The Kinsey Report* or *The Story of the O*. In my high school the stack-read was *Our Bodies, Ourselves*, the puberty manual with pencil drawings of penises and vaginas, corners folded by a lineage of readers (the first probably already married with kids), so that the fourteen year-olds crowding in at the start of every year, could turn directly to: "Masturbation Is Normal," "INTERCOURSE," and drawings of how they all fit together. Or the book on JFK's assassination, the dog-ears bringing you straight to Kennedy on the autopsy table, his head splayed open, brains peeking out from behind a loose bit of forehead, his face looking like a deflated balloon at a little kid birthday party, his eyes, open. Or the book about Marilyn Monroe, this time Marilyn at the morgue, hair wet, slicked back on her head, her face still beautiful, a little sunken, covered in freckles, her eyes, closed. There were some other books in my high school library, too, that were dog-eared for teenage looky-loos. The one about shark attacks where some guy's torso is bitten in half and he's obviously dead, his mouth hanging open, or the one with the picture of Jesse James's side-man petrified in a coffin up in Red Wing (not far from Shelton College), three bullet holes in his chest (you could see holes in his jacket where they went through) or the book about the Elephant Man with his head that looked like a scabby potato. There were medical books, too: warts and lesions, strange growths and rashes on the tongue. The books at the Shelton library were like that, even though none of the corners were turned. It was obvious. That amount of wear and tear didn't happen from being left unread for decades. They weren't dog-eared, but it was still obvious. Maybe college kids were too mature to dog-ear the pages for easy reference. Maybe college kids liked to read the full book to get the context and historic relevance of raping and murdering young maidens for sexual pleasure. Then I began to notice there were a whole lot of underlined sections in a bunch of the books.

Count Valenska _drank_ *the blood with* _gusto_.

I paged forward to see what else there was.

Her bodice lay <u>torn</u> on the floor. His hands were <u>like claws</u>, <u>ripping</u> her skin.

I wondered if there was some message being transmitted from one reader to the next. From one—I checked the register in the back again—Sheila Godrich to one Nigel Hendries to one Arthur Campbell to me.

I went from page to page reading only the underlined parts:

> *Drank gusto torn like claws, ripping situation crenu-*
> *lated removal and destruction standing half-awake*
> *certain repugnance iron pikes and heads dangling*
> (pages 103 – 112)

I didn't understand. Was it a joke? Was it an extended haiku? I would've ripped out the pages for further study and cherishing, but it was too many pages and I didn't want to get in trouble my first week at college for defacing school property. I was never one for defacing things or breaking rules, really. I maybe said bad things under my breath but that was mostly it. Or I maybe did things to myself, like defaced my skin (a paring knife), but that was mostly it, and I wore long sleeves so it wouldn't show.

Then I noticed that some of the underlines were in different pen, as if some of the un-derlines had been added later by readers who had understood. By Nigel or Arthur, maybe, or another someone like me, you know, another lurker in the stacks.

When I was a little kid, Ma and Daddy sent me to stay with Poppy and Nana in Maine. I don't know why, except maybe they wanted some alone time, and Ma was always saying out of my hair so maybe she needed the summer to recover from the rest of the year. I only remem-bered scattered things, like picking dandelions and blowing their white afros across the lawn. I remembered pulling up my socks—knee-highs—over scabby knees and Poppy sitting in the smoke house rolling tobacco. Everyone said, "Hank, old pal, that's a fine little girl you have there." When he held my hand—swiped it, really, from my side—I remembered wondering if people thought he was my husband, not my grandpa even though I was only seven. I wondered if people thought I was his sex slave. I know a sex slave isn't usually something little kids know about, but maybe I was precocious. Maybe it was Nana's *National Enquirer*'s that widened my horizons, or maybe it was innate, or who knows. Maybe in a former life…oh, now I sound like one of those drippy fortune tellers. Have you ever noticed they always wear draped purple things instead of normal shirts? Or like a million turquoise beads around their necks or unicorn pendants or crystal pendulums? Well, they do. But anyway, out there, in the woods with Poppy and Nana, catfish for dinner, or squirrel or deer shank, I wouldn't have been the first sex slave around, that's for sure. Poppy's hands were callused and always a little clammy when he grabbed mine in his. Each fingernail was a mixture of the day's mess. A little something from the car engine, a little something from the liquor store, a little something from the side of the road picking up recyclables to turn in for five cents a piece. He told me not to tell about the five cents, like he was embarrassed. We walked together between the gas station and the smoke house and he pointed at anything that glinted in the brush at the side of the road. "What's that?" he'd say, and I was supposed to run and see. Nana screamed at me when I came home covered in ticks.

"What the hell have you been doing?" she yelled, putting the tweezers in the flame of her Bic (kept in the same corduroy pouch as her Winston's), then squished it into the gut of the tick until it let go.

Poppy shot me warning looks about how I wasn't supposed to tell, so I said, "Chasing Raisin," who was the neighbor's dog, because crossing Poppy had its consequences, and Nana swore some more and said, "I'm gonna get on the horn with those people about that damn canine," but she never did, only threatened, and then settled into the settee with a *Reader's Digest* or *TV Guide* even though the reception was bad out there in the countryside. I lay in the backyard when she was done, and stared at all the clouds above my head. I didn't tell you before but there was this invisible friend I had up there whose name was Claxon, and he was a sort of cloud man, like one of those Roman gods, I guess, Poseidon or something, except he was in the sky instead of the sea. I looked for Claxon up there, and when I found him, I felt okay, felt like all the little red marks where the ticks had me would heal up fine, and the lies I told to protect Poppy were going to disappear, and all the other dumb things I worried about: grass stains and fingernail dirt, the stitch between Ma's eyes when she was mad, the yucky feeling in my stomach that I had even then (the tickle I called it), the slobber of dogs on my hands, stuff like that. I felt like all that would disappear, too. Like Claxon had a wand and, even though it sounds queer to say, he waved it around like magic, like fairy dust (totally queer) until I fell asleep.

I guess I'm thinking of this because it's kind of how it was looking at the underlines in the stack-reads. Like the underlines were Claxon and everything was going to be okay. Or maybe not. Sometimes it was hard to tell.

craig bergman

NAKED IN THE BROOKLYN AFTERNOON

Crowned boobalahs screeching towards Lithuanian nannies. Gorgeous brunette Puerto Rican mamas shimmying booty from the muffin top down. Walkman Johnny at the stoop on 115th & Coney Island Avenue picking up the numbers for the day.

"Hey, mamasita, how 'bout I come over later and tell you the story of my life?" he says to a hot little cuchita sitting by the fire hydrant cooling off her hair extensions.

It's 100+ in Coney Island this Tuesday. The apartment buildings bake slowly in the red sun. The TV man said Mars is the closest it's been to Earth in three centuries and Johnny can feel the energy, the energy of war tussling, pulling, stabbing at his loins. It's worse than usual. His pock-marked face is extra-twitchy as the neurons firing from his balls are going at a rapid-fire pace. His right hand nervously fingers the black spiral notepad he writes the numbers in. The smell of hot asphalt and piss steaming into his nostrils are a twisted inner-city aphrodisiac. He steps past the beat-up grey Grand Marquis parked at the curb and approaches the little chiquita mamasita. He feels this is going to be his lucky day.

"Don't even think about it, Johnny. My momma didn't raise no puta, you muthafucker." "Fine bitch, didn't want you knowing my story anyway," he says, spitting into the ground. He struts off down 115th street, passing under my window, my perch from where I see the whole thing go down. I have a love-hate relationship with this ghost world, where the Russians mix with the local Brooklynites, the spics, the niggers, the chinks, the black-hats, the greaseballs, all boiled up in a surreal melting pot of hatred and ignorant misery. A moment in time, a snapshot of the cross section of humanity where mass meets no class, where it makes me wonder just how many twisted realities there are under this blue dome. And what bent God could have set it all in motion. I look down on the twitching seething swells of humanity pouring out of the sub-way stations, into the bars, out of the beds and into the schools. I look down on the air-conditioning mechanics who come from a day of verbal abuse to crying kids and bitched out wives, come home to take off their belts and take it out on the kids. I look down on the dispos-sessed, the forgotten souls, the shadow figures lurking in dark alleyways, waiting to pounce on unsuspecting little boys and girls, to rip their clothes off and violate the rest of their years. I look down at the cheaters, the slothful, the three hundred pound men squeezing in and out of greasy diner banquets, arguing over checks and bad wait service. I look down at this body, naked in the Brooklyn afternoon, hairy and white, 70 pounds overweight. My once trim, suburban body atrophied, ravaged, by heroin and crack and beer and cheap vodka. I look down at my wheez-ing pimply chest, compromised by discount drugstore cigarettes and black fumes. It's a foul world. He's a foul God. I've almost had my fill of it. That next fix sits on my nightstand. It's all I can do to keep myself from jumping into this shit sea spread out beneath me.

laurel benton

ORANGE CREAMSICLE

what makes a parakeet go insane?
my bird is whacked.
for six months
he was the sweetest,
most docile little thing.
i could hold him, kiss him, snuzzle him,
and he was fine,
but now he's on fire.
now, for no apparent reason,
he's on fire.
maybe he's like me.
maybe his cage
has grown too small.

dicky-bird makes the sound i make
and then he bites.
my taste in men is much too good.
my standards are much too high.

i had an orange creamsicle
for breakfast and a piece
of garlic bread to feed
my deep humanity.
humanity, yes,
not humility. no,
it's not my thing,
but i'm working on it.

teresa died 3 weeks ago.
i'd known her 13 years.
in that time she'd had 3 kids,
2 girls and a boy,
3 angry kids
born into miserable marriage.
the oldest girl, abby, is fifteen.
when teresa's mother died,
teresa was fifteen.
her father was a
philandering incestuous pedophile;

her husband was just
a philandering shmuck.
she caught him in bed once
with his whore.
i'm not name calling,
that was her job.
"caught" really isn't the right word.
she walked into HER bedroom
and found HER husband
in HER bed fucking
HIS whore,
and she did not leave him.
she wanted out,
but she would not leave him.
so she died, not by pills or a bullet,
but by slow poison.
3 years ago the doctor said
it was cancer,
she needed to have it out.
"No" she said, "that's too invasive."
"I'll dissolve it on my own,
and it will be a miracle."
now i'm not knocking miracles.
i believe they happen everyday.
but when she said that,
i knew it was horseshit.
she'd made her choice.
she was OUTTA here.
she was already gone.

anya yurchyshyn

CALIFORNIA

it's not my fault that you never knew it
and only learned it now
california is funny that way huh
your east coast bubble gum snap sarcasm didn't
do you much good
it went out the window when you learned to sit still
oh wait you haven't learned yet

breathe
sit still
it's hard
because you lose a little sense of yourself
people think you're a little much
acerbic really
but it feels good being in your body

get out of elsewhere
stop bumping into things
it's okay
breathe
god's here
in california

didn't you know
he's a hippie
snap
he doesn't live across the street
in the church that you had all your prom pictures taken in front of
he's not your father
breathe
it's okay

it's california
god is here in california
that's why you came
god loves you in california
it's okay to breathe and touch things slow
it's okay to breathe with your hands in your pockets snap
it's okay to breathe and admit that

you're learning.

conrad romo

SCAR

She had a scar on her left shoulder to show me, she promised.
My imagination had it much bigger.
I could show her a scar or six. Many of which were self-inflicted.
She asked how many times we had sex.
"Twice," I reminded her and thought of the word remission.
She asked, "Was it good?"
"Yeah," I said and lied. I fucked her no differently
than any other in my life.
As if it was the desperate last time this was ever gonna happen.
I fucked the way I always did.
Like any second she'd snap to her senses and push me off.
I fucked her like she had no spine.

WOMEN PROBLEMS

"Women problems," is what he tells me. Not that I'm asking.
This is why I don't like going to the Laundromat; these kinds of
awkward bare-chested exchanges. My quarter for his two dimes and a nickel
is what he hit me up for first.
The third time he offered, "I'm having a real bad day...women problems."
Like they were responsible for the stench coming from his body.
Like they were to blame for what at best was mud on the ass of his pants.
Like they had something to do with his false teeth,
and other personal effects scattered on a washer.
He had a couple quart bottles of beer in a paper bag on the floor.
His face has fresh bruises and his nose looks like a cheese grater has
been taken to it. Yeah, I thought, women will do that.

SNAKE EYES

"Wanna see me blow smoke outta my eyes?" Billy asks.
He's the big kid on the block. George's brother.
The only reason he's even talking to me is 'cause one
time he called me small fry and right back I called him big fry,
which made him laugh. I don't know what got into me. Billy is
smoking and pacing in his backyard right next door to my
Granddad's where I've been living again. Billy has a temper I've seen
at times. Like when he smashed a bottle over the head of a stray cat
in the neighborhood. That wasn't all that he did when it was dead.
He said it deserved what it got after getting in their house and
peeing on their clothes. I wasn't gonna argue; besides I'd never
seen a skinned cat before.

I'm ankle deep in ivy, leaning against a clapboard garage. I'm about
to ask him where George is, 'cause I don't know what else to say,
when he goes, "Wanna see a trick?" He tells me to grab on to the
chain link fence that separates our two yards and to concentrate on
his eyes. "Are you concentrating? Hang on to the fence and don't
move. Look at my eyes!" Then he brings the cigarette down
burning my hand and laughs as I try to pull back from his grip.
"That'll teach you to not trust anyone again!" He laughs.

TOTAL IMMERSION

In Antigua, Guatemala, off Calle Oriente, I had a moment.
I was lost, which is normal for me. It was the first day of the Spanish
total immersion program. I was trying my best to be on time.
What happened was just this: the sidewalks were narrow. Two small
people would have to negotiate passing each other.
I'm hurrying along, and notice a
telephone pole planted almost in the middle of the sidewalk ahead of me.
There's a wall on one side I can squeeze by, and the street on the other.
I mentally choreograph my action. I'd, without breaking stride, put one
hand on the inside of the pole and swing myself around not having to
step off the curb. I expected the pole to be rough with a potential for
splinters. But, over the course
of years and many thousands of hands that did what I was doing,
it was worn smooth and there was a shared a moment, and I was no longer lost.

chris shearer

ALEX

Mikey owes a bunch of dough. I gotta tell him how much. I'm hot. I feel like I did last Saturday when I bartended the recently gastric bypassed Marsha Kormac and her husband Brugh-or-something-Persian's 60th birthday. Trying to smile and be the happy bartender guy when my head pulses dead thick with a migraine and I'm so nauseous I can't eat. I can't eat. How many times in my life has that happened? Ever? Am I dying? I'd got the server, Samantha, to get me some Advil, but it took too long. Everybody likes the happy bartender guy, even the tall Greek statue beauty with hair piled up and purple wrap graced about her shoulders who stands looking with big eyes waiting for the words. I look back, but there's too much thick pain between us and she turns and gives up, hips curving away past the dance floor, back to her college roommates and mirrored eyes. Sticky hot. Hot that somehow filters too far into my head. Membranes breaking down. Mikey thinks he's gonna get some dough out of Robin. He hasn't even sat himself down to figure out what he owes in back rent and late fees. Dumb fucker thinks he's gonna take her to small claims court and make some money. Crazy dumb asshole. Sitting at my desk going through almost two years of rent rolls like I got time for this bullshit. Hours more, to go through all the photocopies to clear up any discrepancies. Hours and hours I don't have because one psycho computer programming La Rouche-spouting shit childhood tattooed jackass needs some extra dough to get his lying ass back to Georgia. Gonna live in his car! What a load of horseshit. Robin's gonna kick his ass out of here so fast his nuts will spin. I want to be out of here, too. I want to be someone else. I want to be the drunken poet showing up at dinner parties saying brilliant inappropriate things and drawing sophisticated women to me like flies. My nephew Alex's face keeps coming into my thoughts. His pale skin and bald head and too thin body sticking out of too big clothes is haunting me. He whistles and gestures with Tourette's when I meet him and I see he is not dying easily. I say "Hi Alex, good to meet you." He whistles and murmurs something I can't hear. The chemotherapy hasn't left too much of him for the rest of the world. "Aw, your Uncle Ben's taking you for a walk around the block, how nice," and then I turn to Ben, the cousin I knew most as a thick-glassed child and less as a floundering 18 year old and now as a responsible man. I can't stay with Alex. It's too painful to try. I see him sinking down, slipping away. He looks like Corey did when she was starting to go. I don't know if I can attach myself to such a ship again. Not that I was all that great at it the first time. "I don't know how she does it," Ben says, talking about his sister Sally, Alex's mother. "I don't know how you did it," he says to me. I guess he wants me to tell him. "You just get used to it," I say. "You just pretend that everything is going to be all right," and I know that I'm lying because I don't know how you do it. And then I tell him, "I couldn't really handle it, to tell the truth. When my ex took Corey to New York for treatment at this hospital, I stayed in LA." I couldn't do it. "I mean I visited two or three times in the year they were in New York and I was there for the last three months, but it was too much." I would've been dragged down to never come out. I would have died down there in New York. I saved my ass. Did what I could. I knew she was dying. I knew we were only biding time. Everybody knew it. It was the Eighties and it was AIDS. People were afraid to get five feet from her. I wasn't afraid of that. If I was going to get AIDS from Corey, I would have got it long ago, back when nobody knew nothing. It was the depression I was scared of. The slow grind-down into dirt. The every waking minute knowledge that it was hopeless, that she was in constant pain, that the CAT-scan had shown me all those holes in her brain. I'd like to make it up somehow. I'd like to have a chance to prove that I'm not that frail. To prove I can take it, whatever it is. That I won't turn tail and flee when things look real bad, that I'll stand up and die like a man. I'm sending Alex something this week. Something fun, something he can have fun with. A book, maybe.

rebecca rhyne

DRUNKARD MOST HIGH

I had a party once in law school, and I invited law students and Earth First people and some English grad school types. The main thing with a group like this is plenty of alcohol.

So a friend of mine brings along to the party this kind of creepy patrician law professor named Jefferson Chrysler. I can still do a spot-on impression of him, which involves closing my eyes, tilting my nose into the air and talking out of one side of my mouth with my lips sealed. Here's what my friend Ray said Jefferson said when he got to the party:

"Lots of fresh meat tonight."

Among the actually invited guests was a brilliant loud-mouthed, utterly irreverent, utterly alcoholic, poet named Roz. She was my age and from Texas, but WEST Texas, and anything delicate or blossom-like in demeanor was completely burned right out of her. She was, to repeat myself, loud. She yelled. She was argumentative and smart as shit and a drunkard most high.

So, as this party that had gone quite nicely, thank you, is winding down in the backyard, Roz is in a lawn chair, half slumped, drunk as a lord but still conscious and she's hollering, barely able to hold up her head. I go towards her to talk to her, to check on her, and, as I walk, I see Jefferson moving towards her also.

I bend down to understand what she is saying, her words a drunken inebriated screaming rant. I start to understand when she pushes her palms up to my face, and yells, "Look, I get stigmata. I'm getting stigmata."

And I look with amazement and alarm and see in the middle of her palms, by god, a rosy patch growing darker and darker red, in front of my eyes. As I stare at her most unsacred palms pooling bright color under the electric Japanese lanterns hanging above her, and strain to comprehend that stigmata is an actual phenomenon, I tremble at the utter chaos of a universe where stigmata can come to a drunk, bawdy poet at a keg party, surrounded by beer, gnats, and lawyers, as easily as it can come to an ancient cloistered nun.

Roz's head now turns away from my wide-eyed face to the left, towards the toadish face of Jefferson Chrysler, who, having come with one age-inappropriate date, is, with reptilian focus, now trying to pick up a legally drunk stigmatist half his age.

Now, I stand at a spot where a hostess must prove her mettle. Miss Manners has never stood here. Martha has never stood here. I am alone. I act. Perfectly true to my character, I act.

I do not call out in wonder at this holy sign and fall on my knees in awe, even though I do not doubt my eyes that see the signs of the cross in her hands. I look and think only: This is no time for Stigmata.

I put myself between Roz and her predator, and, talking low , I say, "Don't do stigmata, ok?"

She lurches around me yelling god knows what: curses, poetry, come-ons to Professor Chrysler as he moves to regain his position next to her, keeping up the hit. She is helpless in her intoxication. Too much beer, too much spirit, too much poetry, all pouring through her, oozing out crass and bloody. Somehow as I keep talking to her, "Roz, you need to stop the stigmata, don't do stigmata now," and a kind friend agrees to drive Roz home, Prof. Chrysler's own boozy brain seems to realize that there are too many witnesses to his lechery to try to pull Roz from the circle of those who care for her, and somehow, that night at my party, no poets were harmed.

justin klippel

THE NIGHT BEFORE THE FOURTH OF JULY

The fog is rolling in from the beach.
It creeps over the hills
and swirls atop the street lights.
A sleepless night filled with worry and anxiety.
Where the fuck are all my drug addict alcoholic
friends at?
So many times I explain to myself how fortunate I am
not to be a tweaker, slammer, or an alcoholic.
I just smoke some pot
and a couple of Marlboro Lights is enough for me.
But from time to time I miss those scumbag
motherfuckers!
Two years ago I lit candles in all the churches I
visited in Europe
for those boys,
walking down an alley behind a club at night
with a bottle of vodka in one hand
and a pack of friends at either side.
The sound of boots.
Not giving a fuck!
Lots of slutty girls.
They tell me they found me by my scapula.
The glitter on their eyelids did it to me.
Just flesh, nothing special or meaningful.
So much has changed since the Chernobyl destruction of
my friends.
I no longer get collect calls from jail, visit rehabs,
or hospitals.
My whole outlook on myself and the world has changed.
I look at pictures of me from those days and it's a
different guy.
I am not a ghoul, a tough guy, or a ventriloquist doll,
but on the night before the Fourth of July,
I still miss them.

sofiya turin

NOSTALGIA

I hail
From a land of revolutionaries
White nights, Bloody Sundays and deportations to
Siberia
A land of frost
Lost
Somewhere in yesterday's day
Named
Renamed and named again

I hail from survivors
Sustaining life against odds
Through floods, cannon fire and tyrants
Terror lasting for decades
Hearts unwilling to let go of ideals
Even as they are trampled underfoot
By charging horses
Racing towards unpredictability

I hail from worm filled wild raspberries growing on emerald bushes
At summer homes near deep placid lakes
Where wild mushrooms wait to be boiled into evening soup
And fried up on greasy skillets with golden potato wedges

I hail from the soil of forgetfulness
From which I was uprooted
Long before the memories had time to
Crystallize
Long before I knew the history
Or the significance
Of the statues, palaces, cathedrals and squares
Before I could grasp the meaning of the tumultuousness
That characterized the dirt on which I'd trod

Vanilla ice cream cone in hand
Gray fur hat covering steamy pink ears and silky black curls

Eyes wide open
Sensing that I am part of a world so much greater than me—
A world that refuses to let me go.

carmen esquer

A REAL LOVE AFFAIR

Welynne thinks the cop in the cop car at the red light next to Groundworks Coffee, where we're sitting having lunch, is a cutie. I look over my shoulder and see a dark, clean shaven man with alpha male features, strong ones, like a defined jaw and full lips, and agree.

"I can see you with a cop," I say.

"Yeah," she answers.

In a quick swoop, she cups her mouth with her hand. "Did I just spit at you?" she asks. "I'm sorry."

Welynne asks a lot of questions like this, and often, as she is addicted to apologizing for everything she does, everything she says, everything she thinks and feels, sometimes even when she didn't even do or think or truly feel the thing she's apologizing for.

"I didn't notice if you did," I tell her. "And can you please just stop fucking saying you're sorry? I wouldn't be your friend if I didn't tell you. I promise you other people notice how low your self-esteem is and they're just not telling you."

"I know, I know," she says, looking at her boring chicken salad. She picked off all the colorful parts of it and there's a mound of tomatoes and carrots and bell peppers sitting on the plastic lid next to her plate. I am drinking Gunpowder green tea, already having had my lunch. I had to get away from the office anyway.

"I couldn't be with a cop," I say. "I need more stability than that. Not knowing if the person you love is going to come home. Fuck, I mean, if Sal doesn't return my email within the hour, I feel totally unloved. It's enough to ruin my entire day."

"Did they arrest somebody?" she wonders, only half listening to me.

I look at the back seat of the cop car, but can't make out what's behind there. For the next minute, we both stare at it, without saying a word, her fork dangling midair between her mouth and her plate, my neck twisted all the way to the left. As the light turns from red to green, I realize that what I'm looking at is the white cotton shirt on a heavyset Mexican man.

"That must be the low point in his life," I say, as we both turn our heads in unison, watching the car make its way across the intersection.

I can't help it. I am a little relieved that someone else is having an official low point. Like low points are a normal part of life. I had mine last Saturday just after midnight.

It was at the wedding of Marissa and Manny Juarez in Huntington Beach, a ritzy ceremony that came off more like a prom than a wedding. To illustrate this point, I'd like to bring your attention to the couple's first dance. First of all, homegirl wore a tiara and as they stepped on the stage for their big moment, they cued a spotlight on them. Then white smoke appeared on the dance floor, and bubbles fell from the ceiling. During an emotionally heightened moment in their chosen love song, which I forget because I think it hurts my brain to remember, the groom picked up the bride and twirled her, lifting the smoke around them and covering every inch of that ballroom under a thick cloud.

"I am never having a wedding like this," I thought.

I am simply too far gone into Bitter Bitter Land. I felt like Janeane Garofalo. Always playing the cool, but lonely girl who jus can't fit in. So I drank, then I kept drinking. And then I drank some more until I actually crossed the You Have a Drinking Problem line. I understand those are strong accusations against myself, but the thing is, I threw up all over my Anthropologie dress on the drive home. There, I said it. So it's undeniable even to the queen of denial, me. What can I say? It was a defining personal moment; a moment when I realized that without a doubt, I am my father's daughter. I drown my pain in alcohol. I drink to have fun. I drink to avoid feeling awkward around people. He made a career out of it, exited this world with a cirrhotic liver and a tumor the size of a grapefruit on his hip.

And I don't know what was worse, barfing over my brand new dress or having to take the car to the car wash Sunday morning. I had to apologize to the unlucky guy who had the unfortunate task of cleaning my car, which still had pieces of—I cant even say it—crusty barf. The stuff I couldn't get—and the smell. I gave him a huge tip and then I lied to him. Told him I had given a drunken guy a ride home and that he got sick all over my car! Making myself seem like the responsible designated driver.

That was low, but even lower was when I took my dress to the cleaners, but it smelled so bad that the owner told me to wash it first then bring it back to him. Rejected by the cleaners. That's the lowest of low. That's as low as I can ever go. Me, Carmen Esquer, who likes all things pretty. The hard part is not using this as another reason to lower my head, or apologize for who I am, like Welynne does all the time. The real hard part is loving myself despite all my imperfections. Giving myself a real love affair. I don't want to hate myself anymore. I am tired. I want, you know, the unconditional stuff they talk about. The 'till death do us part. Don't worry kid. I'll get you some of that.

leslie ward

THE GENIUS

It's Friday afternoon and I am at the Apple Store. My iPod is going mental–skipping songs and generally misbehaving—and I am hoping someone here can fix it. The 20-something geek in the green t-shirt waves dismissively toward the glass staircase leading to the second floor. "Genius Bar" is all he is able to muster in the way of a directive. I make my way up the stairs, a knot forming in my stomach. I've seen the Genius Bar many times. It's always busy—black stools occupied, laptops open on the counter, geeks behind the bar and customers in front speaking a strange language, both seeming to understand what the other is saying. Serious discussions about gigabytes, megabytes, hard drives and operating systems float through the air thick with knowledge I do not possess.

As I approach the Genius Bar, I try not to look as out of place as I feel, searching for some clue about Genius Bar etiquette. Do I take a number, stand in a line, or mosey up to the Bar confidently with a look that says, "I need help now"? After a few shaky minutes, I notice the computers on either side of the Bar where I am to enter my name and the reason for my visit. Having mastered the sign-in process, I take a seat and wait to be called. And I get to thinking: "Genius Bar? What in the hell am I doing at a Genius Bar?" Then I realize they don't mean me.

It takes a long time to shed the skin of a shame-filled childhood, even after the skin grows too small and tight and I know in my heart that whoever chose that skin for me had it all wrong to begin with. Even after I have twisted and contorted my way out of that skin like a butterfly becoming, after I have worked diligently, against the odds, to fashion a new skin, a more comfortable skin in which I am smart, in which I am worthy, in which I am capable, in which I am okay, in which I belong, even after the head-shrinking, the medication, the yoga, the acupuncture, the new clothes, the new car, the new job, the food, the booze, the cigarettes and the sex, after all those things there still remains a shadow of a doubt. I'm not sure why, but somehow I know that I'm still not quite okay enough.

Anyway, the first time I ever saw the Genius Bar I thought it must be a special place for really, really smart people to hang out together and have someone to talk to, sort of like a Mensa Lounge or something. I stayed far away, averting my gaze, lest they discover I was a pedestrian interloper in their genius world and order me out of the store, their voices loud, eyebrows furrowed in anger and judgment, a stiff index finger pointing toward the stairs until I would flee in horror.

But I'm still here, watching the customers, deep in discussion with the geeks behind the bar. They are nodding and asking questions I don't understand. I know computers and technology are designed to make life easier, but they only serve to confuse and overwhelm me. I feel alienated by the left-brain-ness of it all. It's like the world is whizzing by my head, and all I can do is duck. My handwriting has become illegible, so unaccustomed am I to the physical act of writing, putting pen to paper.

I feel isolated. What I crave is human connection. But isolation is easy. It's a game I am really good at, only I don't want to play anymore. Even when I win, I lose. I lose time. I lose myself. I lose little pieces of my soul. I lose my place in the world. I want to have conversations face to face, not via email, to see the recognition in another person's eyes when they get what I am saying or confusion when they don't. Connecting with others will remind me of who I am and who I am becoming. It will tell me that I matter and make a difference. I long to be touched. I long to be touched. I want my home to be a universe of laughter and belonging. I want to be my husband's pastime. I want to see light in his eyes. I want to be the first one who hears him. I long to be touched.

Someone is calling my name. I look up and one of the geniuses is looking around. He's looking for me. It's my turn. And as I approach the counter, he smiles, and I relax into the stool that awaits me.

david darmstaedter

LIKE I KNOW HENRY

So I was at the Henry Miller library in Big Sur,
looking at his letters, books, photos on the walls.
You were still smoking at such an old age, huh Henry?
I thought. I didn't have to quit sonny, I heard him
say. Then I flipped through some pages of *Big Sur* And
The Oranges Of Hieronymus Bosch. Not like his early
stuff. More like middle-aged stabbing around with a
self-imposed omniscient mind. God is beyond your mind,
Henry. Maybe, maybe, squirt, I heard. Write another
book or two and get back to me.

GROWN

Strange summer. Kid is always gone. Seventeen. Artist.
Comes home for an hour or two, says things like, Dad,
I know what I'm doing. Shut up. Leave me alone. He
came into my office the other day, sat on the couch
across from my desk and started reading a *'Johnny The
Homicidal Maniac'* comic. I was looking for a number in
my phone book. As I flipped through the pages I saw,
Gay Dave 1-800-BUTT-SEX written in it. "When did you
write this," I asked. "Dad, shut up. I'm reading."
"When?" That could have been two years ago. Sure.
Silence. Then I wrote as he read. I couldn't look up
at his beard growth. Young man. I didn't want him to
leave.

DON'T CALL ME CHAUNCEY BUT...

Digging up dead roses in the garden. Plunging the
shovel in. Right through the rotten roots it goes.
Usually. Today a huge red rose bush still had a little
life left in it. Some green flushed into the dry dead
brown. But I dug it up anyway. The long roots moaned
as I ripped them up out of the ground. Dammit, I hate
this, I thought as the thorns got me, ripped into my
skin. 'They told me to do it,' I said as I fell to the
dirt. I'm on my knees what more do you want? I'm
sorry. I went home early.

SUGLISH

I went to a bar downtown with my wife. She said it smelled
like, "Japanese man's cigarette, like fart, like something
p.u. burning." Her name is Sue. She came from Korea at age
fourteen. They put her in ninth grade English when she only
knew a few words of the language. It was hard to learn so
she made up her own way. She speaks Suglish. She tells me,
I'm a pain on her ass or I get on her nerve. She will point
out some Hollywood poseur and say they are dimes a dozen.
Sometimes she feels like she's stuck on the pins and
needles. She is never embarrassed. It is the way she talks.
She is very direct. The other night while we were making
love she grabbed me and said, "I want least two more
decades use out of this cock." I am more in love with her
as I write this. I like that because some days I look at
her and want to end it all. Dump her. Run away. Disappear.
She would cry then go on. I would die. I would surely die
without her.

WHO KNOWS

I'm too tired to love you, always started with me
thinking, I'm not right for this world. Already at two
or three years old, no, I was screamin' right out of
the chute. Bloody murder mamma. Who is my mamma? You
poor woman, you're just some human that…I can't go
back that far. Was dinner fish or not last night? Now
ya' got me dancin' like a chicken on a hot plate, a
bubble gum chewin' bear. Firecrackers. M-80's. Coconut
covered dates. Stick em' all up your ass. I say. I
say. I say. And again who is that? Too tired to love
you, baby goes way beyond selfish. Please, let me
sleep. No one knows until this life is over anyway.

judeth oden

FASTER FASTER CITY LIGHTS

There was a fucking eight year old kid who wrote a book when I was fucking eight years old about her mom dying of cancer. My teacher was very proud that an eight year old's book was in our school library. She should be proud of me. I wrote a story about a rabbit who ate donuts and talked. I started a new book. A real one. A real big one. A real big live one. And scary too and serious. *Rainbows Never End* about my mother dying of cancer. Only she wasn't really. I was a writer and could actually make up stories. I'd get published in the library and make her jealous, and I'd go on *Donahue* and shock them all because none of that shit even happened.

I know a lot about the world. Kentucky Fried Chicken and the Mars Bar, and Muskeeters and *Wonderful World of Disney*. I learn from my couch and sleeping in on Saturday mornings with the TV running in the distance, scratching my tit.

I like city lights at nighttime and headlights on the highway in rows of white in front of me and red behind me. My eyes make me tired. I can't focus good on lights or words. They all blur. Faster faster city lights. Sometimes I just let everything blur. A lot of times I do that when I'm watching the TV. I lay on my side, and Mr. Cosby's hand all spread fingered in the air, because he's right and funny, blends into Mrs. Cosby's feathered bangs. I got my hand between my legs. I know how to flex my thighs to rub my clit.

Moonshine moon-day moon-night dancing. I got shows. I like the ones we used to watch and the water cooler ones, too. I know a lot of shit, like who Charlie Chan is, that other people don't know. Aunt Rosemary'd always yell at me to quit talking to myself because they send people who talk to themselves to the loony bin, so I talk to my TV. Traffic signal lights blend to make orange and brown dots between the red and yellow and yellow and green. I'm watching about weimaraners. They think they're human and they don't shed. *Twilight Zone* comes on in twelve minutes on the Sci-Fi channel. You'd never guess I'd be one of those sci-fi people. You'd be wrong. The scariest *Twilight Zone* is this one where this boy has to take a test at 16 to qualify to be part of society. Only I think there was another part to it—like he decided to take the test a couple of years early so his Mama would buy him a cell phone, only he needs to pass the test to get, like, a license to use the phone. He takes the test on the computer and he's sweating bullets and big letters come up on the screen, "YOU FAIL," and then you cut to his parents sitting at the dinner table, and the answering machine comes on, and a voice inquires about their son's funeral arrangements.

The best show is *Survivor*. I log onto survivorsucks.com a couple times a day. Because, until *Survivor* goes into syndication, survivorsucks.com is all I have 167 hours of the week. On the site I learned that everyone fits into one of seven personality types. I fall between the cracks. Sometimes I play the shy angle. Sometimes I go for maternal.

I have never been maternal. *Survivor* sucks. It's all sex and bikinis. I never post on these sites. It's good to get your aggression out, but I think it ruins my chances. There are network plants (they call them gophers) on these sites. They don't want me to know what I know. They want bimbos. I can't do bimbo. They call me a lurker. I'm just playing it safe. What do I know, anyway? I don't have any insider tips. This isn't Hollywood. It's my fuckin' living room. I read the exercise logs. ViverLuvr does *Dance Dance Revolution* for two hours a day and swims and lifts weights. They think she's anorexic, but she swears she weighs 140 lbs. There's a whole thread on *Dance Dance Revolution*. They love it. I think I'll get me one. *Dance Dance Revolution*. I should get a laptop, so that I can log on in bed.

I joined the survivorsucks.com book club. I don't post. I lurk. I read *The Island* by Peter Benchley. They said *Lost* was based on *The Island*. I don't see it. I can't swim. That's why they don't want me. Every season I take a different angle. Pick three words. Creative, caring, giving: Maternal. Thoughtful, sensitive, loyal: Shy. Funny, generous, outspoken: Bitchy. I'm the rags-to-riches story. I'm the bored housewife. I'm the unfulfilled artist. I'm the childless mother. I'm the cynic. That takes us through the fifth season. I'm not getting naked on TV. I've heard they're models hired through a casting agency—not on survivorsucks.com but from the non-believers. Don't laugh at me. JoNi1982 who posts, she just passed the Bar. She was met with congratulations. Someone told me the contestants sleep on a cruise ship. They said it's union regulations for the crew to have a craft table and that contestants eat donuts from the table, too. All I know is that they get damn skinny and bug bitten to be eating donuts in a captain's suite.

RealRob who posts on survivorsucks started his own *Survivor* site. I like what he has to say. I joined the site. It's my last chance. *Survivor* isn't going to last much longer. They never do. I have to become part of it now, before syndication starts. It stops being alive then, and becomes part of my living room. RealRob asked me for a lot of personal information. I didn't like that, but I gave it to him anyway. I logged onto the chat room. They all wanted to know who I was. They could see me, and I could see them, but they can't make me talk. I'm a lurker. It's not my thing. They kicked me out. No lurkers allowed. Thought I might be a gopher.

In my head I'm writing a best-selling novel about a serial killer who chooses his victims by their license plate number. It's kind of like that game we played as kids on those long-ass road trips to Aunt Rosemary's, the one where you spell out the alphabet from license plates or that other one where you try to find all fifty states. I found Hawaii once, outside of D.C. The plate's got a rainbow stretching all the way across it. It's kinda like that game, only about killing people. I like to masturbate over my underwear when I'm logged on. The cotton's softer than finger to flesh unless I'm already wet. I love smooth lines. I love smooth feels.

alicia ruskin

TERMINAL

Skidding curbside mad dash to make the gate
First time JetBlue dig the leatherette those seat back teevee screens
I'm coast to coast grown up in kick pleat skirt
Laptop Amex Treo Starbucks New York Times
Count the babies pray it's not a cranky flight
Text Larry kiss kiss eat right work hard
So I won't need to
Gear up to thrust accelerate we rocket into float
Snappy crew pelts the barking seals pre-packaged crap
God it's different
Back when I ached to be a stew
Gorgeous slim hipped platinum french twist
Coddled us across Atlantic chop our big United trip
Spent trying to cut loose from Chartres, Windsor Court
Tongue kissing boys from Putney Leeds Toulouse
Thick furred arms prickling my blouse unbuttoned to the Maidenform
I'm America all innocence and cash
He's crossing borders capturing the flag
Violating treaties I battle to lose
The taste of boiled sweets and clotted cream
Boxed good bye candy tucked beneath the seat
Over Greenwich Dad blips off the radar
Sucked out a back galley door, jettisoned
Screams outrage down the sky becomes
A bobbing gull picked carcass
Mom's tray-table upright bolted in ticking off the custom's list
One tin of tea one cashmere jacket
One child one broken covenant
I gulp a cherry spiked coke from the archangel of Pan Am
And put my head down
Preparing for the crash.

ellen kimmel

ELEGY FOR THE FALLEN AND FOUND

Who has not stood at the edge,
eyes wide open,
watching the self step off?
Who has not jumped with eyes closed?
We all fall with desire.

I stand, alone on the mountain,
overlooking the black stormy sea from where I came.
It is not in the other we are found.
It is in our capacity to find,
in the stepping-off point
when our feet leave the earth.
It is when we seek that our soul is seen.

There needs to be wanting
and we need to reach,
stretch out our arms,
and our arms will extend
like Batia's who saved Moses from the Nile,
like mine as I tell my lover
what I have been afraid to say.

If we open a space inside of us
the size of the eye of a needle,
God will help us find the Heavens,
and when the Heavens descend,
we will hear the sound of the soul of every living thing—
every tree
every leaf
every stone
every fruit
every man
every woman.
Every blade of grass will have an angel
to watch over it and sing,
Grow, Grow, Grow.

We have to fall blind,

hopeless,
and let hope fly out into the sky,
free it from its caged existence
out into the expansive universe.

We need to be free of hope
in order to be filled with it.
We have to empty ourselves
of everything we have hidden,
everything we have kept secret–
of how fragile I am,
of how I have been hurt,
of my wish for tenderness–
even the unknown,
even the un-thought.
We have to be empty to be full.

Empty.
I am empty.
I am fallen.
I am empty.
I am found.

kat popovich

TIDES OF JULY

We awake early from sleep, and it is already hot. The sky stretches over us, vast, and brushed with strokes of white. The air is close. Still. We greet the dogs and cats—eight in all—writhing around our ankles and fill big bowls with water and leave the house for the linen shrouded arms of the coast. We follow the winding road down, past drowsy shops and sleeping houses, into the deserted canyon, with matted hair tracing mad halos around our heads, careening onwards, overgrown canyon walls dwarfing us on either side, our way carved out eons ago by the path of the wind and of the sea. We do not speak as we savor the morning like the last drops of a bottle of wine cradled in a dark cellar for decades.

We settle on a patch of crunchy, virgin sand and lay back. I hear the ocean and I am unborn again, hearing my mother's heartbeat. It calls me back. The sun pulls itself higher into the parched sky, and they begin to come—families, clusters of life, bound by blood and by birth, flocking to the sea, seeking respite from the air-conditioned lives they lead. It calls them too, and they leave the safety of dry ground just long enough to be picked up by a wave and wonder what's below them and if they will get swept out to sea, until they're back on the sand, shivering and feeling alive.

I am coaxed from my reverie by an unseen hand, spindly invisible fingers pulling me up by my collarbone—the shrill voices of children, and looking, I see myself in their tiny knees, their tiny hands, grasping plastic spades and buckets. Their laughter drizzles the salty air like honey, tracing clear paths down the hills of their skin. Their wide eyes hold no pain, show no hint of the sorrow that will bring them one day to their knees. My childhood feels distant and close here. I remember jumping over waves of foam and unearthing fragments of seashells, buried treasures in the coarse sand, where crabs waited to bite my toes. Summer dusks chasing fireflies, bedtime stories and night lights, the hum of the fan in the attic. I was terrified of the attic. In winter the door to the staircase stayed closed, but in summer it was always open and I was always scared. That was a long time ago. I look away.

I turn to the mothers. They are watching their children. I see my future in them. In their ferocious jaws, their tired skin, their watchful eyes. Those fervent eyes, scanning the skyline, alert, ready to pounce on a leaf, a twig, a bug, a man—any threat to the sweet nectarine flesh of their young. Those eyes, shrouded now by dark heavy glasses, meant to mask their fear, but not their joy. Never their joy. I see my future in them. I feel the ache in my belly and in my breast, a strange longing for the weight of that sour, sweet milk. I long to see my future in them, but I can't. I look to the ocean. I fix my hazel gaze on her vast, ever-moving, watery stage, beneath whose dark velvet curtain, the battle for death and life rages on. No eyes close peacefully beneath that curtain. Even in death they remain open, ever watchful and unsleeping. I see my end in her.

niedra gabriel

I WENT SEARCHING

I went searching
        For my way
                to live

Open card appeared on shelf
"Walk boldly towards your dreams"

I felt fear

My dreams are unclear,
Misting change
Mostly—I stroll in the ditch by the side of the road
Wondering what is on that other side

        I went searching
        For my way

Zen Book on my path
I read

When you walk, walk
When you stand, stand
But above all—don't wobble.
    I felt fear.
    I wobble all the time,
I fall
I lose my way, I turn around,
I try to stand—I stumble on.

I went searching,

Wise man sharing
        On the way

Be clear in what you say,
There is power in words,
They will come to be,

I felt fear

What I say will change and shift
From hour to hour, from day to day,

I do not know what I will say
More than naught
What comes to be,
          slips out sideways,
glorious extraction.

I went on

Wise man preaching

You are—lost this way
Throw it all away,
          To find your own—
          Way

I felt anger
Am I not on my Way?
Am I Lost?
I wobble, I fumble
   I often change my mind,

Am I lost?   I am Not ….
          I AM, as I AM

katy melody

DRINKING UP

Eric and Fiona joined us at our table last night for a summer repast of wild salmon and tender stalks of asparagus from the grill, with new potatoes cut in delicate quarters to round out the offerings. Eric, the American life-long best friend of my husband Andy, who long ago fell in love with all things French, but the wine was Californian when he asked me, "More?" the bottle tipped toward my glass. It was my father with his hand-blown, green-crackle apertif glass, the one with two small raisins on the tiny stem, who said, "Just stick your tongue in" to taste the sherry or scotch. "More?" Eric asked and I would stick my tongue in while my father said, "You may not like it." He watched for my response, and when I said, "Ooh I like how it makes me all warm inside," he growled to himself, as if that wasn't the response he'd hoped for from his twelve-year-old daughter. Eric touched the green glass bouteille, the pale liquid cascading to goblet depth and on to splash against tongue, tastes budding in fervent awakening, the eso-phageal gate clicking time while alcohol bred from vintners' dreaming, fruit infusion, atmos-pheric chance of perfection, tempted my arched palate 'til I gladly downed the stuff and said, "Okay, so what do I do? Swirl the stuff around, breathe in, breathe out, what?" And Eric, Mr. "Grew up in the valley (that's San Fernando)…went to Paris, met the french girl, had the half-french kids, lived in Paree and became, that's right, a wine expert," says, "Just drink from the bottle, drink from the true, from the source, the heart of it, pulse of it. Drink, it's your lips that are waiting. Drink, it's your life that wants living. Drink, it's your blood that wants pulsing to rhythms not found in the dry stalk of yesterday's planning, of yesterday's planting, of yesterday's wanting. You're wanting not getting. Must make for the bottle, want mother, no mother, must learn to obey. Learn to nod and say, 'Yes, I want that, will you give, can I have, yes I want.' Will you say it? Oh, when. Will you have it? Oh, when. It's not yours 'less you want it and ask—no. not ask–'less you take what's given, what's offered."

There's a problem with that, with hiding and waiting. All the learned behaviors, the sig-nature stuff. I've done it, could do it in languages I don't even speak. It's universal, saying, 'I'm not worthy.' I'll take the discounted attention, the remainder bin notice, the last bite of salmon on my plate, and I asked, "Does anyone want this, I won't eat it." There I was at our table, small, the rest of the family gone, dishes cleared. I leaned my chin into my palm and stared down vegetables that were part of the "everything" that I had to eat on my plate.

Andy reached over and took that last bite. He makes me dinner almost every night, grills, sautes, tosses. He makes me dinner at night and our bed in the morning. He makes me happy. I feel self-conscious saying that. Don't we all know that one person can't make another person happy. Maybe it's because I want to find that deeper mirth, the imp, the forest sprite that lives down below in the mossy glen, the forgotten land to which I've sent her. Yet, she is ever alert to play in all its forms and messengers whose call wends between the layers of dark lati-tudes to her eager heart. Her laugh breaks all restraints, defies the bans I put on her. She's her own, a wild one, despite my tethering. Like Macy dancing while I play the broken kiddie piano.

Or Fiona and her bracelets, bright-colored metals, her eyes excited past language when I show her the decoupage boxes.

I've got to stop asking why. There is no good watch lies the ticket stipulates geronemo leap halsayhasay. It's a beat bitter. All thighs and no butter, what's a girl? Acid pushups, harang the harlot, religioncool no buttah, swatchit, this time it's for bake and shakeit, bake 'n settle the water, our horses yonder, no but-ah, s'what I'm sayin'? Peony beggars untoward the rest, pasture view Roll'emBoys. S'fantastic, he's sleeping. It's dogs that won't lie down, my studious fronting yesyesbut, nobut, nobut nobut ahhhhhhhhh. See what I'm sayin'?

Nekkid girl, oh you may sing if you want to, find you must sing, sing every breath, make your song all your saying, the saying of one who has all the keys. It is past time for unlocking, past time for the knocking, no time for the hushing that comes from your door, time is now to drench in the sweat of the shit that makes you happy, you know, the cannolis, the root beer twin pops, the blow-up pool for two. Quit with the insights. Woohoo f'you. Quit lookin' at the yard, and get the fuck out there. Eat a tomato and shut the fuck up.

robert carroll

MY NAME IS ROBERT
(after Walt Whitman's *Song of Myself*)

"Hey Walt, wait up
I've been looking for you.
I found you once when I was a boy
sixteen, strapping, full of hair
the Ann Arbor air so tasty
the breeze
the ride down the hill to the Huron River
the trees
a riot in reds, golds, and greens
their leaves
flirted with the light rays' raptures
on our way to the old Dexter cider mill
the donuts hot
with grease
the juice icy cold
we barely saved our seared tongues.

I do not know you
but I know you and love you
for your mulchings and droppings
your blades spring forth in multiple eruptions-
slivers, slips, and vines-
flowers
wild and dark and yellow.

I've been looking for you Walt.
Once I thought I found you in a fuzzy-faced friend,
a man whose eyes were blue and wide and twinkling.
I thought I found a brother, another like me.
On the beach we shared stories and sang songs
but it all turned wrong.
Did I want too much?
Do I want too much now?

I've been looking for you Walt
in the Cascade Mountains' majesty
Yosemite's half dome
the sulfur springs of Yellowstone,

Niagra, Dakota, and the Black Canyon of the Gunnison River-
walls so close and sheer you can't see the bottom from the top.

I looked for you everywhere,
and my mother gave me *Leaves of Grass*
but I couldn't find you there
spread out as I was
and tight
and tense
as a stone.

But now Walt, it's different-
all different and the same-
The illness and the dying, the belief decayed
a dust ball balled up behind socks in a corner
and yet, here you are, rumpled in trousers.
The grass stains the soles of our understanding
Walt, and so when at fifty
I heard your voice call
I knew it was time.
We must talk.

I know about your father dying
and the white hot heat
the plumb bob straight and true
and I know death
and I'm a seeker, too.
　Anyway,
I wouldn't hide anything from you-
not hairs nor hemorrhoids
not lisps nor lost teeth
not tongue nor cheek
not lies—
not even the bald-faced ones.
I want you to know me Walt
and remember me.

I've been looking for you Walt.
I've searched
I shined
I shed light where light cuts out
positive to negative
north to south
man to woman

man to man
the beggar on the street
holier than I'll ever be
the monks in white satin praying
the leaves saying, "Yes, take us,"
and all the while the children are dying Walt.
My father is dying,
and so am I
and you
and all the ladies and gentlemen
who all have to go sometime.

Indulge me this:
You loafed and called to your soul.
Today we hang out, but no one abides.
You and I span the centuries Walt
and you're right.
You are me and I am you
and together we are a chorus of electricity.
I hear you Walt, and I love you.
I bring you forget-me-nots and hope
not for me
though God knows I need salvation
but for us.

Now that I have found you
we will stroll a while linked
by blood and conversation
atoms and particles
intercourse and time
spirits in communion
our souls unshod
the green world agog
our eyes scintillating visions
our voices yell from the rooftop, Yawps!
the new millennium needs us Walt
before we say goodbye
my friend
before we say goodbye
again.

kathleen matson

THE END OF JULY

It's California gift show time, where wholesale buyers in the THOUSANDS from spas and hotels and gift shops all over the country convene in Los Angeles and my own life has gone away and I eat and breathe books for special markets and personal care and table top items like little tea pots with silver chandeliers on them or cups and plates with "choc-o-late" written in script all over them and the buyers are lousy examples of human beings, and I have to start reading books on Buddhism in order to get through my repulsion to them.

I am reading about Buddhism, only because the Random House Shambala distribution was weeded out before the show. "We want pictures, not words," say the buyers, and I saw a bright yellow cover that said START WHERE YOU ARE and thought hmmm, I'll take that. I get free books and free creams and free lotions, an obvious perk. Some of the staff question how much I help myself to and my answer is hey, the boss says take as much as you want, it's not stock options, it's hand lotion.

Pema Chodron, American Buddhist nun, presents century old theories of how to allevi-ate suffering, this theory being to lean into the pain which is the opposite of what we, as hu-manoids, do as a practice. She claims it creates an opening for stillness, an opening for tender-ness, an opening for compassion. I figured I've tried everything else, why not, so I start applying it to the middle-aged fat-assed tight-lipped trend-wearing streak-haired luggage-dragging illiter-ate pinched-nose buyers I am required to engage with during the show (did I mention I LOATHE them?) and it had a positive effect—on me. I actually saw immediate results. Where before I would feel these walls go up, say to a young blonde from Palm Springs with hair down to her ass, wearing a truckers hat and Goth makeup, and skull rings with a trashy Southern accent get DEMANDING with me, I just watched my horror, my resentment, my repulsion (didn't say it wasn't still there), breathed that in (these are the instructions) and breathed out good will to her, and check it out, I was able to connect, not to her, to me. I, the all powerful wizard of oz, I, the expert, I, I, I the rolling stone who would have checked her off my list, eeeeeuuuuuu, FREAK!!!!, asked her name again and she said, "Corrine," and I said, Oh, I love that name, years ago I picked it to change my name to and she said, with attitude, "No, it's Corin," and she spelled it. "C-O-R-I-N. Yeah, my grand daddy told my mama she should name me Corin because I was the core that was in her."

Would I have expected that from her mouth? Hardly.

It opened the gap like magic.

The Corrine I named myself, the Corrine I was becoming, was really Karen, accent on the first syllable, like Karen Blixen, my writer mentor, the woman I wanted to become in my old lady years. Hmmmmmm. Why I see it that way is another question, and I've had no time to write and was down for the count with food poisoning the first two days of the show which was horrible, but it let me stay home to watch the food channel and TCM all afternoon and even though I was sick I was still fascinated by Paula Dean's double chocolate gooey sticky pudding.

I keep looking behind me for something to hold on to. I keep looking for something to ground me, and now I've begun to read Buddhist practices and I can't go back, and everything is uncertain but the light in your eyes, and I laugh at my smallness and I lean in toward the sun sparkling on water, my mother's garden in full bloom in summer, the way the grass smells after it's freshly cut, fireflies through cornfields, the tall old sycamores that grow deep deep green in July and give me what I need. I lean in toward what hasn't been written, toward that story, open, in a notebook on my desk, at chapter 16, at nine thousand words, at something I do not know the answer to and maybe never will.

What came before is prologue, I lean in toward the blue sky, the yellow light, the spring creeks, and the mountains, and the bears, and the magpies.

It's gift show time, and my own life has not gone away. I lean in toward the interior of the flower.

jack grapes

TIME TO DANCE

There's too much time to sing,
and not enough time to dance.
The sea is for singing, the land for dancing,
and the dog that will not die
does both.
My grandfather told me this
when I was 12 and he'd been dead for thirty years.
My grandfather on my mother's side.
My grandfather on my father's side, we don't know
when he died, having abandoned the family
when my father was two.
I'm writing this down
camping by the Kern River,
where there are no watches to measure time or distance.
Josh does his dance by the tent
and Lori notices that his feet move like my feet,
meaning one of my grandfathers
still speaks and moves through him.
This poem, then, is a song to my son,
and to my wife, and to my friends,
who do this dance with me.
And I am grateful for the kind of richness
that refuses to be turned into art.

Trees, then rocks, then mountains, then sky,
then clouds, then God, who forgives
me for knowing He doesn't exist.
Still, I thank Him for all He's given me,
nothing I've dared ask for, nothing
I would have dared pray for,
but not a day goes by that I don't send up
little balloons of thank-you's.

When I made my birthday wish,
which we celebrated last night around the campfire,
I wished for each one of my friends
a life full of everything God has given me—
a God who doesn't even exist.

He hears our songs, He accepts our dances.
And sometimes I wonder, especially at night,
if He will punish me and take everything away,
a punishment I'd duly deserve for my lack of faith.
I'd like to say to Him,
I believe in You, You are there,
but I can't.
He knows how badly I want to be able to say this.
But I know what I know.
The truth will not go away.
The unspeakable things we do to each other and to the children.
Job asked Him for a reason and was scolded
just for asking.
Imagine the gall—to question The Creator about the world He created.
I don't deserve my good fortune,
yet accept it without question.
My wife, my son, my deep and truest friends
who love me.
And it's all too much to hold or carry.
There's so much to sing about,
I've hardly begun to dance,
and there's so little time to dance.
I would dance. I would dance with Him who gave me so much,
but would He dance with me?
Would He open his arms and follow my lead,
me, who dares not question,
who receives and receives and gives
Him nothing back, not even a question directed straight at Him,
not even the heartfelt supplication
of one small prayer.

tim simone

PORCHES

Like dew exploding for the benefit of light, like a mouth full of dirt, like a penal yard stare, I let it dangle in front of my shoulders. I'm embarrassed by my feet; I walk around barefoot all weekend, stepping on sharp crystals flung from a factory of urine and shit. They are all fucked up, my feet. Quiet I sit. When I hit this, when I hold the lighter over the bowl, left thumb on the carb, facilitating the miracle of miracles, all the empty spaces, all of them bowing, scraping, shying away from the entirety of the atmosphere, covering now the lone house at the end of the cul-de-sac, covering the children racing their father to the swimming hole, covering the earth from the immensity of the heavens, from a clenched hand releasing its left thumb to steal, to stare unblinking in a vacant theater, in a private box, at vision after vision materialized in echoing lungs turned black and twisted, all for a few hours company, all for companionship. To take in the likeness of old friends, laughing and calling your name over a dark field drenched with warm suds—'cause Anderson forgot the ice. Suds spilling from plastic cups tipped in the wake of tight virgin bottoms squeezed by adolescent hands burning, still burning with last night's cum pounded out to the rhythm of wet lips crested with salt and suds, the rhythm of pale flesh in the stolen moonlight, in the stolen columns of smoke ripped through water and glass. Calling your name again and again with mirth, with jealousy born of ignorance, lacking in sophistication, lacking in malice, boiling over with the desire and the knowledge of the hand, sour and sweet, that you'll let them smell. Or the prized dangling latex filled with rivers of future as promising as mine is now on this empty porch. I require peace. Not thinking of all the doing that should be done or did or didn't do, I let my head dangle in front of my shoulders. Quiet.

Sometimes it's the smallest of movements. Turning my head it occurred to me. In that small movement, things came into focus. I noticed the contrast of his fiber thin hair, his pale scalp against the slanting morning light. Sitting there beside Jack, my massive hand, for him, an attractive offering. His outstretched grasp swallowing my pinky whole, stabilizing those fat naked legs. It occurred to me how amazing it was that this baby boy, who only yesterday abandoned miles of fine white sand, who departed the Florida coast, the Gulf Coast, this baby boy Jack who only yesterday was so far from me, who only yesterday stood with his mother, my sister, now stands with me, sharing the waves of heat rising over the blacktop beyond his grandparents' porch. Sitting here it occurred to me how far away I am now, from him. It occurred to me why I'm still alone.

Old man, I pray, with your white beard and glasses, how did you get this far? How did you arrive at the corner of 84th and 2nd in your pressed khaki's and ox-blood shoes? Drinking your coffee, glad-handing. How do you do it? Standing, hugging, laughing – remarkable! What makes you so full of life? When the women embrace you, I imagine scalding espresso dumped into your twinkling eyes. I don't believe you're happy. Why aren't you lying in your own filth?

Why aren't you in some soft stinking chair? Why aren't you hiding from all these beautiful woman? Why doesn't your heart fail when they pass you by? Do you feel alone? So alone that you'd do something, anything for a few moments, for a few hours company. Why aren't you praying for an anchor? Why not all that instead of your nod, your expressions, your stare, your familiar affections. Why not that instead of all of your racking and pummeling. If you told me you could handle it, that you were not afraid, I would let you reach me. If I was a man I'd lay it before you. You could probably help me. Old man take my hand. Stop me from hurling this baby boy from his Grandparents' porch.

Letting my head dangle in front of my shoulders. Holding your hand, Jack. Holding my lungs full of green burnt gray then black. Feeling the retreating emptiness. Watching waves of heat over the blacktop, I see. I am frozen. I cannot feel your grip, your slight tugs. You never existed in the place I am now.

Dottie do you see me hunched, twisted, tiptoeing by your door – look at how petrified. Holding my lungs full of green burnt gray then black. Holding your hand. Mary, do you notice that I'm coughing and making noises so that while you sleep, you'll know I'm near. So you can steal yourself, so that dirty hands won't soil your body, so you can ward off your monstrous brother. Molly, do you believe the story I'm reciting about all the countless nights I slept outside, because I refused to walk up the stairs past your room, because the comfort of my own bed was rarely worth the quickening of your heart? Outside Grizzlies tear flesh from my bones. I don't care. How could I ever blame you Dottie? Heroin's forever filled your empty spaces. I get that. Mine are never completely gone, but then again, I was never as bold as you were. It would have been nice if, before you died, you had known I didn't hate you. That would have been real nice. If you had known I was as afraid of myself as you were of sleeping, that I'm still as afraid of myself as you were of Pat. That I would never do what he did, that I'd never lay a hand on you, and if you had known that death was not your only option, then maybe some day you might have believed I didn't hate you. He is my flesh. He's my blood, and there are gallons of black magic in that. It's time I lit fire and ripped columns of smoke through water and glass. It's time to cover the empty spaces. It's time to chase you around the house, to play hide and seek, to bait a hook. To lay a rose by your body, to watch Mark kiss you goodbye and wish I had thought to do that. It's time to just sit, to sit on this porch and forget about my potential.

francine taylor

AFTER THE MASSAGE

Brown skins with white smiles draw warm baths:
Herbal bath/tonic/Please ask for assistance.

A woman, beyond Rubenesque,
 (I imagine her to be so much for the right man.)
buoyant above the stone bench,
outlined with foam,
accented with clear bubbles,
arms splayed across tiled edges,
bicycling her legs gently nowhere.
Impossible to distinguish
how much on her plate,
how many kids trailing behind,
how fat the wallet.

No clothes, no organizers
or jewelry to tattle on any of us.
We're all here to relax,
whether twice a week
or once a year luxury.
Relaxed.
Relaxed.
Back to the world we're escaping,
credit card slip signed and tucked into my jeans pocket,
I wonder about plastic surgeon ads
scattered amidst the pages of The Weekly,
the cost/risk factors associated with breast augmentation.

What we're all given.
What we're all left with.

marianne franco

THE ROOM

Walking up Gramma's driveway I kept my head down, slid my eyes to the corners and peeked up to the second story. Nobody, not even my dad, had been up there in fifty years. Just as I remembered, there were white curtains and long windows, long enough to imagine a full body with a bloody face staring down at me.

In the house on the first floor was my angel in waiting, yes, Gramma in the kitchen sitting in her sunny spot at the head of the table, the wallpaper and the floors still yellowed and cracked, the cross above her head watching over her.

"Hi Gramma," I yelled across the room holding my son, Michael.

"Where's his socks?" she said.

"What? No hello, no how are you, no come stay?"

"Where's his socks?"

"How can you see? You're legally blind, Gramma."

"You have no socks for your son?"

"I have socks in the car, Gramma, but it's 100 degrees outside."

"A baby needs socks. He can't go without socks. Go get his socks"

"Okay. Okay. I'll go get the socks."

Gramma put down the rosary and took Michael on her lap. On my way out I snuck a butterscotch from the candy dish on the credenza. I peeked in one of the drawers. I dialed 9 on the old black rotary phone. The door creaked to the china cabinet when I opened it, and I touched all the china. Something about this house made me a sinner. Yeah, maybe God dominated here, but when I came for a visit, the devil saw an opportunity to move around.

In the cellar I stood under the low ceilings and stone walls. I checked for loose rocks, thinking I'd find hidden money. Everything was just as I remembered: the grape press, the fermenting barrels, the wine bottles. I've told Gramma that I want this when she goes. But everybody wants something from Gramma. So she's never agreed to anything.

I took another set of stairs that led back to the kitchen.

"Where are his socks," Gramma yelled.

"I'm going. I'm going right now," I said. I ran for the door next to the sink. Ahhh the pantry. If heaven was a health food store then the pantry was hell. I remembered the days when this was full of panetone and pizelle, candy and cakes and my favorite anisette cookies. She'd offer me one and I'd sneak three more into my pocket. Mmmmm. I could smell the ghost of them haunting all the boxes of macaroni.

As I sniffed I turned and what did I see, a crystal door handle poking between a tall stack of empty sauce jars. This was a first for me, seeing another door in the pantry. I restacked the jars to the side and turned the glass knob. I pulled and pulled and on the third pull the door shook and opened. Oh my God, it was a room no bigger than 6 feet square. Light diffused through dirty lace curtains: a rocking chair, a hutch and a whole lot of dusty clothes. I found a secret: Gramma's private room off the side of hell. A room where she pulled the pin from her braided bun and unbuttoned her blouse, where she read letters from her mama and cried for home. This was where she was safe, safe, Jesus forgive her, to hate her husband.

My home, my life, my God was missing a room like this. I was tired. I was sick. I was pregnant again and it was too soon to tell anyone. How was I going to work at my job, nurture this unborn, be a mother to my baby and a wife to my husband and still try to achieve my dreams? If only I had a room in our small house, with a room like this where I could let my secrets out of their chest, a space to be weak, a time to be vulnerable, a place to shut the door and keep all my love for me.

I looked around Gramma's room for something to steal, something as the first brick to building my own room. A picture, a painting, a piece of paper with her handwriting. I settled for a spool of thread, blue thread sitting upright on the windowsill. I slipped it in my pocket, snuck back into the pantry, out the porch, past the garage and down the driveway. I forgot why I was going to the car. Oh yes, socks. My son needed socks.

lisa becker

SEPARATION ANXIETY

I never paid much attention to the horror stories my friends told me about their kids starting pre-school. Somehow I thought their tales of separation anxiety were a bit exaggerated. I mean, what's the big deal? You drop your kid off, give them a kiss and pick them up 5 hours later. As long as you come back there shouldn't be an issue of abandonment, right?

Wrong. With kids, nothing is as easy as it sounds. We visited the pre-school three times to lessen the blow of the first day. One of those visits happened to be the same day as Emily's 3rd birthday so Scout walked right into chocolate cupcakes with sprinkles, fresh strawberries and juice boxes. "I like pre-school, mommy!" Scout said walking back to the car with frosting smeared all over her shirt. "Today was a special day because it was Emily's birthday," I said. "They don't serve cupcakes everyday at pre-school, honey." She grinned at me like she was possessed by the devil and said, "I like pre-school, mommy!" Okay, she's on some sugar high and not hearing a word I say. Thank God the next time we visited the snack was raisins and string cheese.

She got to pick out her own backpack and lunch box and the first day of pre-school was built up with the same excitement and anticipation as Christmas morning. There were photos too. She put her backpack on which was half her size, held her lunch box with both hands, stood on the front porch and smiled the same way I did for my mother every first day of school.

As we walked up the ramp to her classroom, I felt her grip tighten around my hand and her feet get heavy and slow. "Don't worry, angel, Mama's gonna stay for a bit," I said guiding her in the front door. Josh was out of there in 7 minutes, but I stayed for a bit…an hour…okay, an hour and a half. How could I leave? Every time Scout saw a kid fall apart after being dropped off, she would give me that look and say, "Mama don't leave." I watched the teacher, Miss Martha, comfort the kids with hugs and change the subject. "Come over here, and I'll read you a story," she said in her motherly, Brooklyn accent. Within 3 minutes, the crying stopped. At least half the kids had some adverse reaction to being dropped off and Scout took note of each one and kept looking in my direction. One little girl even threw up right into her father's hand. He rushed by me to the bathroom carrying vomit in one hand and his screaming daughter in the other. I must have looked shocked, because Miss Martha acted like it was no big deal. "Oh, that happens everyday with Amanda," she said smiling. "She'll be fine in a minute." Scout saw the whole thing and wanted to sit in my lap. My cell phone rang. It was Josh. "You're still there?" he said surprised. "Yeah, I was just getting ready to leave," I said, "…but Scout won't let me out of her sight."

He started in, "Honey, the whole point of her going…."

"I know, I'm leaving as soon as they go out to the play yard," I said cutting him off. I turned off my phone and thought…it's so easy for him. Miss Martha called the kids over to a red line on the carpet. They all held on to a rope and sang a song as they marched out to the play yard. This was my chance to break away. Scout's never met a slide she didn't like.

She won't care that I leave now, right? Wrong. "Mommy, watch me!" she squealed from the top of the slide. "Wheee!" she sang all the way down and climbed up again. I watched another mom peel her screaming son off her leg and make a break for it. I cannot be the last mom here, I said to myself. I'm stronger than this. Scout's ready to slide down again. "Mommy, watch!" she said smiling. "Okay, honey, one last time and then I have to go," I said looking for Miss Martha. Her smile vanished and instead of "Wheee," she cried, "Nooo!" down the slide and grabbed my hand. "Don't go mommy, don't go!" she cried. Miss Martha was right there and turned to me and said, "Whatever happens, you have to keep going. Remember, the quicker the goodbye, the better."

"Don't worry," I said, "I won't renege on you." I kissed and hugged Scout and told her I'd be back in a couple hours. Giant tears were running down her cheeks as Miss Martha picked her up. I went out the gate and gave her one last look before I turned and walked down the foyer. I could still hear her crying, "Mama, don't go!" I felt sick to my stomach.

I saw the mom before me hiding behind a pillar with a Kleenex to her nose. "Did Ben stop crying?" she asked dabbing her tears. "Uh…yeah, he stopped right after you left," I said. "Oh thank God," she said squeezing my forearm and bowing her head. "I swear this is killing me!" she said breaking down again. "I know, it's hard on all of us," I said trying to comfort her. "There are still two moms out there, so you're doing great. Give yourself some credit. Ben is fine." "Thanks," she replied before blowing her nose.

I started walking to my car and every cell in my body told me to turn around and go back and check on my daughter but I kept going. I looked back only to see a trail of fresh blood dripping behind me. I felt like a vital organ had been ripped from my body and left behind on that playground. By the time I reached my car my eyes were ripe with tears. I got in and they erupted. All my friends were right. They didn't exaggerate one bit. This is a big deal. But I'll have the mornings to myself, 3 days a week. This is a good thing, especially with a new baby boy coming. I can devote the mornings to him while she's at school, and it's great for her development. Hell, I might even get to write a little bit. It's a good thing, right?

jeffrey burton

FALLING

I am getting on to a 737. There are women dressed as flight attendants standing off to the side. There are men in ball caps with headsets in their ears. They are rigging lights and microphones. I walk down the aisle. One of them, a stocky guy with a ponytail, stops me, saying he needs to tape down a cable. An effeminate man is seating the passengers. He waves at me to come forward, hurry up. I look down at the guy with the tape and shrug.

"Grips," he says. "We always have to wait on the grips"

"Bitch, bitch, bitch," says the ponytail guy.

He finishes, and I move further down the aisle. The Bitchy Guy grabs me by my shoulders.

"You. Okay, you go… right…here!"

He sits me in an aisle seat in about the middle of the plane.

"There! How does that feel?"

Great, I tell him.

"You look good. Very business like. Very west coast. Is that a silk suit?"

No, polished cotton, I say.

"Is that your own? Or did we get it for you?"

It's mine, I say.

"Well it's very nice. Nice tie. I love Frank Lloyd Wright."

I went to school there.

"Where, the place in the desert? Oh, those big manly beams. It's so macho. I just love it. Sorry dear, got to get back to work." He turns and starts seating another passenger.

All of a sudden there is a commotion at the front of the plane and in walks Jack Nicholson. He is dressed in a Flight Captain's suit. He takes his hat off to the two flight attendants, "How you doing dears?" He kisses each of their hands and walks down the aisle, greeting passengers.

"I'll be your Captain for this flight. Of course, you realize I've been drinking all day, but not to worry. I've offset that by taking all sorts of non-prescription medication."

The passengers laugh. He comes to me, shakes my hand and leans in. His black hole iris's gleam into mine. Madman faced, he lowers his voice, so only I can hear.

"Don't worry, we're all gonna die."

Vampire white smile and he continues on. I look to my left and realize that one whole side of the plane isn't there. This is strange because I didn't notice that when I was getting on the plane. I hadn't noticed it the whole time I was sitting there. There are cameramen on cranes. The Director sits in his canvas chair giving instructions to an assistant. This is a movie set.

Jack is now in the cockpit. The plane begins to pull back. I look to my left the side and that side of the plane has returned. People are startled,

"He's not really going to try to fly the plane is he?"

We take off. We are flying, wobbling in the air. People get out of their seats and rush toward the cockpit. I try to follow, but I am too far away. The aisle is blocked. The plane drops. We are falling. The plane is diving. All of the sudden I see ground approaching as if looking from the very front of the plane. We are going to crash in a field.

So this is why I've always been afraid of flying. And I know I mean not just crashing but this particular event.

The field fills my view.

Everything goes black.

I'm sweating. It's noon, and it is already hot.

What the fuck? I get up out of bed, walk out into the living room and turn on the wall unit. I'm wool-headed boat deck walking back to bed. Why the fuck would I dream something like that? I'm not going to be flying anytime soon. I've been done with the Dallas job for months.

Mind, stop torturing me, and let me get some fucking sleep. I lay down on my side and close my eyes.

Would you please just let me sleep?

Tired.

Sleep.

Falling.

Asleep.

Tired.

Falling.

Ground.

Down.

It is September 8th, 2001.

katharine paull

PLACEMARKS

I think the last dead tree has toppled for this season.
I have firewood to feed the masses
on frigid Russian days.
I am endowed with plenty,
more than I know—
luscious, swelling vineyards that give no grapes,
leaves that dapple and twine
into nests that harbor low borne life
suckled by barren soil.
I dwell in the matter of lonely things.
I dwell upon the hybrid plantings.
I dwell among the scattered droppings of the earth.
I picked up a mimosa flower and examined
its pink string hairs and sweet smell.
It was a hot, humid afternoon there in the shade.
I stuck the flower in my book.
I didn't know the luxury
of lying under a tree.
I was ignorant in my protected world
bound by pines and corn fields.
I felt safe in the confines of that piece of land,
the salt of the earth that curled in its own froth
and covered the house at night
to preserve and mummify us
in our tight twin beddings
in our solid seeming fortress.
The last time I saw that place
someone had cleared it of those boards
that leaned into one another.
The magnolia tree that had come of age was gone.
I helped choose that blueprint from a book of "L" shaped house plans.
I felt powerful in that place,
embraced in my father's womb.
He perched in a squat upon a railing on a Saturday afternoon.
He wore a white T-shirt,
khaki shorts, and a baseball hat.
He was screening in the porch.
He was young and eager.

paull

He was ambitious and charming.
He was handsome and capable—
the Great Provider.
That's what I thought then.
But we crumbled like that house without him,
like pieces of cake we scattered,
as if waiting to be rebuilt into something solid.
And I flew as far as I could go,
landing somewhere
dry and dangerous,
where I could set my own clock
and dig my own holes
in a dry barren spot.

carrie white

SOMETHING IN THE MIDDLE OF ME

Something has happened
in the middle of me.
I have folded up.
New rolls protecting my torso
that I have fed to ignore where I am.
My life is reshaped by what eats me.

> *No love songs in my ear*
> *No one holding me near*
> *No bikini this year*
> *"You're just aging my dear..."*

I don't sit straight anymore
in the middle of me.
I am fading,
fading off the chart
of sex appeal.
I walk without attention
to the middle of me,
where I am trapped,
where I grieve,
grieving his leaving,
this gut padded into isolation.

> *No love songs in my ear*
> *No one holding me near*
> *No bikini this year*
> *"You're just aging my dear..."*

I used to fall in love easy.
Now what I've used is falling out of me.
I coughed up the bladder of my vine
and pretended
but I am forced to demolish
the middle of me,
the house that raised five children,
the space I shared with husbands and lovers.
This is fear.

white

This is courage.
I don't know what to expect
in the middle of me.

>   *No love songs in my ear*
>   *No one holding me near*
>   *No bikini this year*
>   *I'm just aging my dear...*

I am having a hysterectomy.
Can I be casual?
My youth is in my spirit.
My strength is in my heart.
My love is in living this life.
My hope is always in starting over,
without complications,
without something in the way
in the middle of me.

tim silver

TIME AGO

I hold back until the sun is down,
the summer sky still light,
then pad barefoot to the darkening kitchen,
put ice in the glass, vodka, spirits,
carry them out the side door,
around back, to the empty yard.
There are roads to be taken among memories,
but they lose direction, become unknowable,
like rivers in forests where we swim awhile
and drown. I do not know towards
what numbness the cold current lures me.
The moon lies down on the surface
and disappears among the clouds.
I sit in the old wood chair behind the house,
a light bending over my shoulder,
I raise the glass to my lips,
and wait.

jamile g. mafi

THIS PRETTY PICTURE

I pay an ex-soap star to shrink my head.
Work on the anger,
then I buy a new T.V. and count how many
days I won't go out to pay it off—
seven nights of not going out for cocktails
will pay this big silver box down.

I am addicted to the Myspace stalking.
Checking on all the two-faced people I know
and the pessimism grows.
I call friends to check on my true nature
because I'm not sure anymore.
I'm not sure if good is actually good.
And what of loyalty or honor and what
about actual words...
The news is talking about cheaters.
Yes, I have had my share.

The house is getting clean for the first time in a year.
The office, too.

I'm just racking my brain when the image of
the little old lady at the Costco gas station pops
up. I'm pretty sure that someone that old should not
be driving. Her bony shaking hands maneuvered the
large gas pump to her car. I wanted to help her, but
feared it would be taken the wrong way. That she would
feel that I felt she was feeble.

Her skin hung like drapes. Her purple blonde hair stood still. Her
fingers were adorned with rings. Her neck glistened gold
and all I could think about is—
Where are the full-serve gas stations?
What has happened that someone this old
is by herself,
pumping gas,
trying to save five cents on a 105-degree day
in the middle of Burbank.
And what has happened to me

that this is all I see.
It's thundering in the middle of July.
Small raindrops hit my cheeks as I walk
from the office to the house.
The solid air pushes me away from my destination.
It shifts my mind to places I have shoved in boxes.
Bits of a past that my heart doesn't feel.
Bits of me
that I don't recognize.

It's sunny and raining
and five years ago,
there was a day filled with the same thick air,
filled with a lover napping on the grass,
unfazed by the outside world, content to kiss
and hold hands
on a balmy summer afternoon.
I remember this pretty picture,
that perfect moment,
but I don't feel a thing.
There is no loss, no love, no hate,
just an image that I can describe
on a piece of paper.

maria cristina jiménez

RUINS

"Look at the architecture," the guide says.
"The Incas used no cement, no mortar, no iron."
She holds up a manila envelope
to nudge it between the stones, but can't.
I slide against my lover, arm against arm, leg against leg.
That's how close I want to be. To last through all our wars,
our love sustained. Earthquake proof.

Our guide leaves. Now we can kiss,
pledge our love in this sacred site.
Instead he goes to a corner to chant.
I sit down to meditate.
Llamas walk between us.

We stay till closing. The last two people in the ruins.
I buy postcards and take them down the hill,
on the bus, on the train, on the two planes back home,
all the way to my refrigerator.

I see Machu Picchu
every time I need something to eat,
every time I sit down and write,
every time I ponder the mystery of why he left.

THREE GOLDEN APPLES

My favorite character in Greek Mythology
is Atalanta. The fastest runner
who dared any man to catch up with her,
to keep up with her. The one who beat her
did so by tricking her with three golden apples.
I told you this story. Later you surprised me
with three golden apple-shaped candles.
I was so smitten. So impressed. So easy.
I let you catch me with
Bed, Bath and Beyond.

BIRD WATCHER

He hasn't called.
He's moving away.
He's distant.
I stand alone in this embrace.
I wait for him to hold my hand at the restaurant as we walk out.
I don't want to remind him to hug me, to call me, to go down on me,
to have sex, to touch, to cuddle at night and when he wakes.
It's too late. He's under my microscope.
Now I watch, take notes, compare.
My eyes used to be soft. Now they're ruthless.
They observe the landscape through invisible binoculars.

We just arrived from the Amazons.
I'd use his flashlight to scan the jungle.
I got really good at spotting birds, beetles, walking sticks,
grasshoppers dressed as leaves, spiders hiding under the foliage.
He once asked me how I did it,
how come I was so good at finding all these animals.
I told him I just look at what's in front of me
and notice what's moving out of place.

RSVP

I know I shouldn't do this
but I wonder if you think about me?
Or are you already over me?
Do you miss my ass? The wake up kisses?
How I'd scream "no" when you left in the mornings and you'd laugh?
Our Boggle tournaments? Our hugs?
Sugar, do you miss me?

One time we made love in front of a mirror.
You kept saying how beautiful I was.
Not to me. To my reflection.

REVERSE NAMASTE
(The dark in me bows to the dark in you)

I'm not really sure why we're breaking up.
You said you're confused, something inside of you shifted.
You no longer feel the same way towards me (asshole).
That's OK, I understand.
You said I was the healthiest woman you've ever dated
(motherfucker), so unlike the others.
I love to hear stories about the others
cause those bitches you dated were insane.
I love it when you start with the dark gossip,
God, not even US magazine compares, tell me more.
And tell me more about how sweet I am, how open hearted,
you said I'm the most amazing woman you've ever dated (son of a bitch).
What the fuck is wrong with you? Don't you know who you have by your side?
Don't you know I'm a catch? Don't you know I've never had an STD? That I've
never been drunk? I don't do drugs? I love sex, to give head, swallow?
What's WRONG with you?
I'm sorry, what? Yeah, I understand.
Yeah, yeah, take your time.
I love you too.
Namaste.

WISH YOU WERE HERE

After our breakup you left the pictures
of our trip to South America under my doormat.
I purposefully stepped over them, closed the door, and walked away.
I'll leave them under the straw volcano.
One day, the next tenant will unearth the remains
to discover evidence of a happy couple somewhere far away.
And wonder—like I do—what happened to them?

I BECOME WHAT I WRITE

I become hate when I write in anger.
I become love as I think of what we had.
I become forgiveness as I try to let you go.
I become a hypocrite as I pretend to wish you well.
I become myself the more I go inside.
I become powerful in embracing every emotion.
I become surrender by realizing I'm truly powerless.
I become everyone else cause we've all had our hearts broken.
I become us as I write this poem: short, heartfelt, over.

christy dusablon

A LONG LONG WALKWAY

1.

I've given up on you, mom.
I've given up hope that you'll ever change.
You're a worthless cunt and
I am glad I never came out of it.
To get me out they had to cut you open and then sew you back up.
Now sew me back up, mom,
make me better.
I want to forget that you hid the glass
under the table as I walked through the door.
Would you like to know my secrets?
I'll lay them out for you and let you hold them for a while.
Dad's asleep? You didn't want to fuck him, huh?
Here's a secret: fuck your husband.
You should know how to cum by now.
But I couldn't say it.
I could only ask: "Why's the cup under the table, mom?"
The room was dark.
I could not see her eyes, but I could imagine them,
glazed over and full.
She hated me
for seeing that glass,
for knowing her the way that I do:
pathetic and sad.
"What are you talking about?" she asked.
I decided not to answer her
and walked upstairs.
I walked away.
I always walk away when I know I need to stay.
I'd like to forget
that I find my mother sad and pathetic.
I'd like to forget about completing college and
fornicating uncomfortably.
The presence of my unraveling wits
are too much,
even for keys in the ignition.
Off, not on.
Parked parallel and wanting formation.

It's hard to get comfortable in such an amorphous life,
but I fell asleep anyway.
When I woke
I found my mother on the couch.
I wanted to love her the way I did at ten.
When she was there and
I could find things in her to envy,
like her generosity and patience.
I never thought she'd look at me
with such jealousy;
like I am becoming and she's fading.
The sun aided my feeling of abandonment.
I felt precious and, once again, craved to be held against her breast.
To suck life from her bosom and
fill up
with a life of my own,
a life that dips and takes a breath
when it's suffocating in these pressing walls.
I am choking on air.
I am choking on every lie she's ever told me.
I am choking on these floors and the smell of her hideous breath.
I am choking on the words to forgive her and I am leaving.
Yes, I have decided to leave. School starts soon.
School is my excuse to start.
I can leave
without her condemning me. I am her only friend,
she's never said it, but I am her only friend.
She has no one.

2.

Love: a tipsy turvy stroll down a long walkway.
A long, long walkway
with sparrows flying by and
bells serenading a kind of
soft ballet,
yes a soft ballet,
but on the tips of little toes
that sting at times,
but always find their peak;
the highest possible spot on the mountain, then what?
I'll tell you what:
love is like cheddar cheese. It starts to get old and grow
fuzzy green mold and
who wants moldy cheese, right?
Then the solution becomes as simple as folding laundry,

except well,
laundry and cheese are laundry and cheese.

"I love you," he says.

It's morning and my eyes are little slits on my face.
I can feel how bright he is
with his perfect head nuzzled in my tiny breasts.
Love he says and
here I thought
I was only cheese

I turned over to over think
his words,
to determine my exact purpose in this man's life.
To determine why it is I can forget everything
I've ever believed in if he asks me to.
I could feel the top of his hand moving over my body.
He doesn't care that I don't respond
He touches me between the crack of my ass and
I don't make a noise.
I decline giving him notice of my pleasure.
It does please me, though, his hand in between me,
all over me.
      Mindless.
      Compellingly me,
      persuading me,
      making me his prey,
      his lover of ecstasy,
      serious sober elation
as he ravishes my thighs
      and lips,
      my thick hips, and I,
      biting his mouth   with my teeth
      and making him bleed
      and drip
      red
      onto the nape of my neck.
I can hear him mumble.
Oh!
He needs to be cuddled
when he wants it
and touched
when he wants it and

anything when he wants it
and I,
well I give it to him,
because
this is love, right?

leda rogers

LESSONS

great times were when I
downed six glasses of
scotch and water (tall glasses)
at a weekend drunk party I went to
while studying acting in
new york city.
"have you ever had scotch before?" this fag
asked me
I knew he was…
he didn't know he was…
he didn't know I knew he was…
but he
was
a fag

anyway he handed me
a huge glass of scotch and water
I downed it in one gulp
"how do you feel?" he asked
"fine, I'll have another"
all these guys (mostly fags) and I
proceeded to drink the weekend away

after swallowing
5 glasses of the stuff
I stood up
turned around
asked where the bathroom was
walked in the direction of the hallway
stood there for a moment
and fell flat on my back

it's good that I slept through
the whole damn weekend
whether they wanted to
admit it or not
those guys were only
interested

in picking up
each other
I thought I was going to
find love
that weekend
even though I knew
they were all fags

funny how your mind
tricks you
especially
when you think you're
straight

I was lying to myself
just like those
son-of-a-bitch faggots
only they still looked
at themselves
in the mirror

aeroplane

BY THE HOUSE SMELLS LIKE OLYMPIA

Inside my chest it's green maybe like moss
He never stares never looks never
wants
Please watch
In his hand I would sure to melt a drop swirl
maybe he thinks I steal his good blood
that's why I'm his whenever, but he never wants
there's a tiny brown tear in his sock and his song makes foot-spells when he walks
I can't help but want to follow, but the swallow-me-ups of my hallow, now fullah moss makes
me skip
oops stop
Please watch
No but I watch the bones in his fingers play screws like they were
Some kinda country waiting to be blown up No wait
I meant some kinda fine strange rare guitar
No, like exotic instrument he is so fine and yellow and pretty
But in his house I'm just

ERIK KRISTENSON'S DEAD

erik kristenson's dead
he died killing people
i play my guitar
at least i have something to believe in
outside there's palms and cars chasing cars
it almost sounds like the desert ocean
debbie wants to be a star
but mostly she just gets beat up by cops playing robbers
do you know how lonely it is
always starting over
do you know i once got a dollar
for being so sorry or was it pretty?
do you think i could climb to the center of the brown and scream drown down dyin' universe
and roll it over with my little pinky if i
smiled just once big and dirty
but eric kristenson's dead and he died killing Afghanis
but me i'd rather play act like i care and have no feeling

PINK TOE NAILS
7/20/05 afternoon

it's 2:40 and I can see the end of me
my toes are pink and the red flower rooted just don't speak to me
the dishes are washed but not really
the day is hot so it don't move me
I like what I got but still can't stop the scratch at the walls clocks ceiling tops incessantly my
head's a counter top I just can't wipe clean
If jesus were around I'd slap him on the ass and say, "Look what you've done to me"
You see my toenails are pink and I can see the end of me
It's lits like 2:40 and the red flower rooted just don't speak to me
Hmm, humph, I don't know what you expect from me
It's hard to not get up or maybe that's just my head stuck in permanent bed
so I think
I'll scratch at the wall tick tock and top some [me]
Wonder why the world don't move like I want it to
Maybe baby it's just you've all lost your rockin me waltz groove... tea with cream? or
It's 2:40 and baby you just don't speak to me...
later

[whatever]

STRANGE THINGS TO DO

Strange things to do
When you're
An
Insomniac...
Call the cell phone company at odd hours and
Harass them about bad ring tones, service
etc, in a very friendly voice
I can always feel other people ['s stuff]
But I can't
Feel
My
self.

THURSDAY 143PM
July212005

The table by the window speaks of senseless things
When I cracked the egg open something happened to me
Fire fire fire, fire fire fire, jumping from the seat
And there that table by the window speaks of senseless things
My mother was in Waco the night before she dies every time I tell her to not wash me from her
mind little droplets fall in lavender buckets that I cannot mine out the diamonds that I want so
piggy greed bad to find just some little daddy to call MINE
now hotel 6 in mid-Atlantic porch sea built in the middle of the ice burns when the water is
cold and the neon glow attracts only the waves and gulls and lonely nights
I swear I wouldn't be here with only a chef a maid and a rabbit
some where in the motel 6 mid-Atlantic thinking of fire fire fire and that table speaks of sense-
less things my dad only whispers to the cement wall and the lapping sea ashes....

lucy mccusker

WHAT'S PANTS?

I help my mom into bed noticing that she needs a bath.
She smells like vinegar.
I go into my room
and put two pills on the computer top for
the late night pain.
I feel like taking a few pills myself.
I smoke a few bowls
and wonder when
I'll smell like vinegar
and yell out in pain,
when I'll forget the names of my family,
forget who I love.
I wonder when I'll sit in a chair and not know where I am,
not know what a chair is.

She looks at her socks lying on the floor.

"Take off your pants," I say.

"There, there they are," she points at the socks.

"No, mom, your pants."

The socks are lying next to her white sneakers,
the only shoes she'll wear.

"There..." She's still staring at the socks.

"Mom, your pants." I tug on the leg of her pants.
"Your pants!"

Her eyes meet mine.
"What's pants?" she says.
She really doesn't know.
"What's pants?" she asks me again.

"These," I say and tug on the leg again.
She's wearing black running pants with white stripes down the sides.

"These are your pants."

She sits still, looking at them now.
She hasn't run in 20 years.
She can't even walk.
But there she is—in running pants she cannot even identify.

"Pants?"
She says the word as if it was another language.

"Pants! I never knew that!"
She looks at me.
She wants me to tell her pants is a new word I just made up—
"They used to be called blah blah's. Now they're called pants."

But I don't.
I tell her to just stand up out of her wheelchair
so I can get them off.

"Time to put on your nightgown, mom. Let's take these off."

I pull on the pants again.
She stands up, hips clicking as bone rubs against bone.
She braces herself on the arm of her wheelchair.

"Nightgown?" she says.
"What's nightgown?"

christina kerr

ROSEBUDS

Although the wind was not very strong, I noticed that the top branches of the palm trees on Sunset Boulevard were shaking. Lori and I were sitting on a bus bench, but not going anywhere. I wore a red bandana in my left back pocket, and Lori wore a blue bandana in her right back pocket. Today I was a Blood and Lori was a Crip. Some days we belonged to the same gang, but often we liked to pretend we were on opposing sides, and we'd have to sneak away to be friends.

My breasts had just begun to sprout into rosebuds, and Mom told me I was ready for my first training bra. Lori was one year older than me and her breasts had already developed into full bloom flowers. Lori wore a grown-up bra, but sometimes she didn't and when she wore a white t-shirt without a bra each nipple looked like the center of a sunflower. She would try to impress me by doing things like drinking toilet water, or pretend to be a belly dancer twisting topless in front of the bathroom mirror. I didn't know how to tell her that she only grossed me out. My hair wasn't quite blonde but not quite brunette. My cousin told me once that I have dishwater hair, but I had no idea what she was talking about because I didn't realize that dishwater was a color. Lori had shoulder-length pure yellow hair that always smelled like corn. She had bangs and I had none and my hair reached the middle of my back. Lori had beady blue curious eyes, and mine were almond shaped, somewhere between blue and green. Lori had pierced ears, but Mom told me I had to wait until I was thirteen before she'd take me to the mall to have them done. Once Lori tried to pierce my ears with a needle she'd sterilized in the flame of a gas stove, but the pain was so severe I passed out on the kitchen floor. She threw ice water in my face and said she wouldn't be able to finish the job. Lori had hips and I had none. She went to public school and I went to Catholic school. Lori was my best friend because she was my only friend.

We shared an order of French fries from the All American Burger a few weeks ago and found out we have something in common: we both hate ketchup. We've been hanging out ever since. I'd never seen a Blood or a Crip, but Lori's older brother (who went to Bancroft Junior High) seemed to know all about gangs. Bunny and Cassandra stood on their designated corners and never paid much attention to us, and I pretended not to notice when one of them was being picked up or dropped off by one of their clients. Bunny had a mouth like a candy heart or a flower petal or some kind of little shell, and I wondered who she was when she wasn't standing on her corner. Like how long did she look at herself in the morning when she washed her face. Cassandra didn't appear, not even from a distance, to measure up to Bunny's standard. I wanted to tell Lori I found my mom's pot. But she'd probably ask me to prove it, and I wasn't feeling up to proving anything: the sun was so hot it felt like it had burned the air inside of me, or that my skin was burning from the inside out. I didn't know what I was looking for when I found Mom's pot in her light blue fire-safe lock box, but there it was shiny like a treasure, along with Zodiac papers, a rolling machine, a roach clip, an ashtray she'd bought in Victoria, B.C. and a fancy miniature pipe with a purple stem and a silver bowl. Satiny on the outside. Stained with tar on the inside. I thought about taking the pipe just so mom would know that someone else had been there, but I left everything as she arranged it and let her hold on to her secret box. You know what I think: if she didn't want to get caught she would've changed the lock combination from 0-0-0. Lori would stick her thumb out into traffic when she saw a cool looking car. No-one ever pulled over though. I guess they were more interested in Bunny and Cassandra, and that was fine with me because if a car had ever stopped, I probably would have jumped in, as if I were biting the apple of sin, and said, "Take me to the beach."

The Friday after Thanksgiving Mr.and Mrs. Bradley went to visit Lori's brother, Scott, at a juvenile detention center. Lori said it wasn't a jail or a prison—just a place he'd been sent away to because he'd been caught too many times for stealing old ladies' purses, and the last woman he snatched from was eighty-two and fell to the sidewalk and broke her hip. Scott ran even though he heard the old woman screaming. He took the wallet from the purse, which had twelve dollars in it, and then threw away everything else into a dumpster behind Bank of America. Somebody sitting on the patio at the All American saw the whole thing and called the police.

It was nine in the morning when Lori invited me over to her house. When I got there she was wearing a white t-shirt without a bra and boxer shorts. She asked me what I wanted to do.

"I don't know," I told her.

She put on her brother's Jethro Tull album and went to the kitchen and brought me a glass of orange juice.

"Drink it fast. The oranges are a little bitter."

Lori didn't warn me that the orange juice was in the glass only to distract me from the taste of vodka. I couldn't finish it and almost threw up what I'd already swallowed.

"Lie on the couch. In a few minutes everything will be fine." She handed me another glass. "Drink it slowly, don't sip it; just take small tastes like you're eating a piece of butterscotch candy or a strawberry or a Peppermint Patty."

"It's making my stomach burn."

"That's the best part."

I did what she said and finished my second drink of the morning. By the time I finished my third each sip of vodka tasted sweeter and sweeter.

We left the couch and started dancing to "Aqualung" as loud as the speakers would handle. Lori took her shirt off and ran out the front door. The sky was just a bit lighter than the blue boxer shorts she was wearing. Inside, the room started spinning and my stomach felt nauseous and I was too wobbly to rescue Lori's nakedness from the front yard. Mr. Hermann across the street called the cops. When I saw the squad car pull up to Lori's house I hid under a bed.

Her brother's bed maybe, I don't remember, just my face on the carpet that smelled like the bus bench next to Bunny's corner on Sunset Boulevard. I fell asleep as if I were sinking to the bot

tom of an ocean like honey mixing with cement. I didn't answer when the cop yelled, "Is there anyone else in the house," but he found me anyway. When he woke me up, he didn't even have to ask.

I said my name is Cynthie Johnson. I live at 1400 North Genesee Street. My phone number is 855-8181.

He called Dad who was there in five minutes. While I waited, I sat back on the couch with my head between my knees. I counted my toes one by one by one, only to make sure I was still all there. Dad carried me the two blocks to our home, just like how dead people are carried in the movies.

chiwan choi

FABRIC

two weeks away from marriage
i'm standing in front of the mirror
wearing nothing but her black panties
as if this is how i can carry her with me
while she eats pulled pork in charlotte
and waves goodbye to the swimming pool
to the girls in love with pale guys in glasses
to her pink room with the slanted ceiling
that i used to dream about 25 years ago
in los angeles.
my body looks ridiculous like this
the small pretty shiny fabric over my dick
making the rest of me look
undone
misshapen
weak
and it makes sense.
this is who i am
this is who i have always seen
my skin is so yellow
i liked it so much more on the streets of paraguay
shirtless
and feet bare
but all that is temporary
we hold our curses dear until the end
my yellow skin
the empty pages that never stop

there was a vanity in my mother's room
i was four
and i found her bras
and i thought the cups were perfectly shaped
to cover my ass cheeks
and that day i started putting everything on my skin
chocolate
silk
hands
blood

shit
corpses
prayers
dirt
and i feel it again
the breathing around me
the pounding hearts of beasts unwithered
and i hold my breath
contort my naked body until it looks like winter
i want to fuck everything
i want to fuck everything
that knows about death
until i have touched enough of the surface of the world
to know that
it is enough to just
have lived
a little while.

bios

AEROPLANE. Please change all those "coulds" to "can" e.g. me, always setting myself on fire, me who can never stand still, me who can never stand to be pre-tty, me who's always me.

ALAN BERMAN teaches web, programming, and office applications at El Camino Real High School in Woodland Hills, CA. He has been published in *Mosaic, Literary Magazine Review, Guitar Review*, and *VUEPoint*. He lives in Los Angeles.

ALICIA RUSKJN recently returned to writing and realized she loves it as much as she did when she was just a girl. This is the second time she has appeared in *Wednesday*.

ANYA C. YURCHYSHYN is 27 and moved out to Venice Beach, California from New York three years ago after graduating from the Gallatin School at NYU.

CARMEN ESQUER has traveled the world chasing the magical and has settled in Los Angeles to write. She has read original stories and poetry around the city and makes a living as an editor for a teen magazine.

CAROL JOFFE is a woman of varying ages and discernments. She has had a couple of husbands and several careers, including Extreme Mothering. After doing extensive work in the area, she still has an aversion to death. Currently she lives in L.A. and spends her time rewriting things she has already rewritten.

CARRIE WHITE is a mother of five, a grandmother of eight, a lifetime Beverly Hills salon owning superstar hairdresser, a professional photographer, a published poet with an autobiography in progress, a chemical dependency recovery speaker for 21 years, a world traveler, and a student.

CHIWAN CHOI is Los Angeles, by way of Paraguay and Korea. He is a founding editor of *Wednesday*, this incredible magazine you are reading, and author of two books of poetry, *dog-fuzz on the asscrack/time out of space* and *lo-fidelity lovesongs*. He has returned to Los Angeles after receiving his MFA in Dramatic Writing from the Tisch School at NYU. He lives with his really hot wife and two weird dogs.

CHRIS SHEARER is an enthusiast and lives in a building in Los Angeles. He is an actor in a whole bunch of films that nobody ever sees and he is not bitter about it. Some of them weren't so good. The last one is great. It's called *In This Short Life* and Chris is hoping other enthusiasts will go see it. Chris grew up in the back of a pickup truck in upstate New York and believe me, it's cold enough to freeze the nuts off a squirrel up there. Fuckin cold, man. Green, though. Some-day he will have a house up there – one with a heater in it.

CHRISTY DUSABLON is a part-time waitress and a full time student. She is a sister, daughter, granddaughter, and great granddaughter. But more than anything she wants so badly to be a classic writer.

CHRISTINA KERR, an avid *I Love Lucy* fan, was born and lives in Los Angeles. She's married to a very understanding husband, and is a mother to a wise and spirited long hair Chihuahua.

CONRAD ROMO is a native Los Angeleno. He is the producer of two dynamic short story and poetry reading events: *Tongue&Groove* & *Palabrazilla*. He is short, stocky and swarthy. He would like to be thought of as a ladies' man, a man's man and a dog's best friend. He makes his daily bread selling stuff and is slowly compiling a collection of short stories and a CD.

CRAIG BERGMAN thinks he's hardcore New York, but he's just an LA poet who likes to wear a Yankees cap and remember the good old days in Coney Island and girl watching in Brooklyn when he didn't have to shed so much blood on the page.

DAVID DARMSTAEDTER has written five screenplays (one of which is currently in option) and has been recognized as a valuable actor and poet for many years. His most recent work, a novel entitled *My Monster* was previewed as an excerpt in the first issue of *Wednesday*. Currently, David is working on a book of short stories and short poems.

ELLEN KIMMEL is a social worker who has been studying poetry for over ten years. She is originally from Brooklyn and Lawn Giland. When she is not writing poetry, she is throwing pots at the Bitter Root Pottery Studio.

FRANCINE TAYLOR is a writer who has lived in Los Angeles since 1987. She has worked in the film industry and has written screenplays, fiction, non-fiction and poetry. She writes regularly for greencine.com, an independent film website, and loves talking to independent film makers. She is thrilled to be included in the second issue of *Wednesday*.

JACK GRAPES is an award-winning poet, playwright, actor and teacher, recipient of numerous fellowships and grants from the National Endowment for the Arts and the California Arts Council. He's the author of 13 books of poetry, and also wrote and starred in *Circle of Will,* which ran for several years in Hollywood and won drama critic awards for Best Comedy and Best Performance by an Actor. His most recent book is *Lucky Finds*, and a spoken-word CD, *Pretend*.

JAMILE G. MAFI was born and raised in southern California. The daughter of a Persian/French immigrant and an Scott/Irish American mother, she is still plagued today with the eternal question of which hand should hold the fork?

JEFFREY BURTON has won numerous awards for his work in securing the airports after 9/11. The experiences from his work fuel the stories he is compiling for his novel.

JUDETH ODEN was born in 1978, a fact she likes to rub in her husband's face now and then. She is addicted to *Millenium* on DVD. She has enjoyed success as an off-off-Broadway playwright, has an MFA in Dramatic Writing from NYU, teaches an arts and literacy program for high school students, and is a founding editor of *Wednesday*.

JUSTIN KLIPPEL is a native Angeleno. He is 24 years old and a student. He plans on becoming a history teacher. He loves intensity, 1950's pinup girls, and shamanic tendencies.

KAT POPOVIC came to LA via Ohio, Australia and Indonesia. She can swear in five languages, loves to dance naked in the kitchen, and wants to be buried at sea (but she has two more continents to visit first). She lives in North Hollywood with her husband and their four creatures.

KATHARINE PAULL, raised in Churchland, a once rural community in Tidewater Virginia, has been transplanted to Kagel Canyon, an unincorporated community in the foothills of Los Angeles County.

KATHLEEN MATSON grew up in Ohio, studied in DC, and now writes in California, but it's really the Montana hiding inside her that she wants to get to. And somewhere in the pages of her novel-in-progress, there is a map hidden that will show her how to get there.

KATY MELODY is a writer and psychotherapist. She lives in Los Angeles with her husband, actor Andrew Parks.

LAUREL BENTON is a Valley Girl born and bred, and still living in LA (because the natives never leave) and when she was 19, she marched right up to Gregory Peck and shook his hand because he, after all, WAS Atticus Finch.

LEDA ROGERS conceived the term "eclectic creator" to describe herself. She loves to go rock hounding for semi-precious stones with her dog Scooby. This Actor, Writer, Graphic Designer, Silversmith, Brooklyn original, now lives to create in Los Angeles.

LESLIE WARD was born in 1958, in Lincoln, Nebraska, moving to Los Angeles a year later where she has lived ever since, save for a brief stint in Colorado where she fell in love with the mountains while diligently honing her waitressing skills. Leslie continues to live and work in Los Angeles, selling big books with pretty covers, lots of pictures and very few words. She lives with her wildly talented artist husband, Gary, their unbelievably adorable son, Henry, and their fabulous dog, Ed.

LISA BECKER graduated from San Diego State University with a degree in Marketing. She is a production supervisor on feature films and is working on her first book. She's been published in the anthologies *ONTHEBUS* and *Wednesday* and is the author of 4 chapbooks. She lives in Encino, California with her husband Josh, their daughter Scout and stepchildren Ethan and Kendall. Contact her at FrauLisa@aol.com

LIZZY WARONKER grew up on an island. She's writing her first novel.

LUCY MCCUSKER is a native Angeleno and has been a hair stylist extraordinaire for a long ass time. She is currently trying to put together the million crazy stories from her life into a novel so the Hollywood types holding guns to her head can steal it and make buckets of cash.

MARIA CRISTINA JIMÉNEZ is Puerto Rican, Yoga teacher, poetry lover. Currently addicted to Sudoku and Boggle. More will be revealed.

MARIANNE FRANCO was born in Boston, MA, in the middle of five brothers and sisters. She went to Emerson College to study writing for film and television. She is the author of a book of poems, *A Rag Doll's House*. She now lives in Los Angeles with her husband and son.

NIEDRA GABRIEL lives in L.A. by mistake. She grew up in Israel, traveled the world and came to the USA motivated by a life long quest to find and express herself. She has been a professional Jack "of all trades". This expansive and challenging career provided fertile soil to plant and grow the tree of her choosing called "Living the life of your Dreams," where she built a tree house and lives in a gloriously impractical manner. Writing is the branch of this tree where the swing hangs...

REBECCA RHYNE, now practicing law in Los Angeles, is from Texas where she learned to plant okra.

ROBERT CARROLL is a psychiatrist and poet. He has published more than thirty chapbooks of poetry as well as articles, chapters, and stories. He was a member of the 'Los Angeles Performance Poetry Slam Team' and has toured and read nationally. His current interest is on the healing powers of poetry. He serves as Vice President of the National Association for Poetry Therapy.

SCARLETT RILEY is a newly converted Los Angeleno who came from a vineyard, the San Francisco Bay and a black lab with a white paw. Her favorite moment here in the South was telling a stranger, "I'm the wealthiest person I know and I'm overdrawn in my account."

SOFIYA TURIN. Words are her lifeline, her breath, her air, her water. Each word is a petal, each sentence a flower. Bouquets are created, every time pen kisses paper. Plugging into the silence she brings forth life from the vapor.

TIM SILVER was born and grew up in Ohio, journeyed in Europe, Africa, and Asia, studied film, theater, and literature in London and New York City. He works freelance in film and television production. He lives with his wife, Margarita, in Santa Monica, California.

TIM SIMONE is a Bostonian who loves Buffalo Fingers, beer, and an occasional smoke. He is a founding editor of *Wednesday*. Tim has recently begun reading his work on numerous stages across the underrated literary Mecca that is Los Angeles.

CPSIA information can be obtained at www.ICGtesting.com
Printed in the USA
BVOW11s1440050915

416533BV00004B/12/P